Keyhole

I0695128

George Morrison

Tennin Books™

Author: George Morrison
Title: Keyhole ™

Copyright © 2023 by George Morrison
Location: Wisconsin, USA
Publisher: Tennin Books
Publication Date: July, 2023
First printing: 2023
ISBN: 979-8-9886326-0-3 (pbk. book)
Subjects: Fiction, Science Fiction, Humorous
Book cover design by Aymen Klidi

T his is a work of fiction. All of the characters and events portrayed in this book are either fictitious or are used fictitiously. Any resemblance to persons living or dead or who might be inclined to sue me is purely coincidental.

(This page intentionally left blank.)

1

"You're late with your payment, Nick."

Nick stepped back from the colossal biped blocking his path. Barely a meter-and-a-half tall himself, he scarcely reached the waist of the being in front of him. Even if Nick had been the same size as the thug, he'd have been no match for him. Nick's tidy potbelly, round like his head, bespoke too much beer and too little exercise, whereas the goon's arm muscles threatened to burst the double-XL sleeves of his suit.

Dressed in a pink pinstripe suit and a fedora that clashed with his necrotic yellow skin, Urk's top debt collector, Durkin, was well-known to Nick. And, given Nick's recent bad luck at the casinos, the thug's visit was no surprise.

Another of Urk's enforcers blocked Nick's progress as he stumbled backward. Swallowing hard, Nick licked his lips before answering.

"Please, Durkin, I'll have Urk's credits by next week. Payday's only a couple of days off. You know I'm good for it. Just give me more time."

The thug leaned over, grabbed Nick by the neck, and squeezed. Hard. Water from the planet's perpetual mist ran down the sleeve of the mobster's suit, mixing with the tears running down Nick's face. His native world, Ghoul, was a desert planet, and his aversion to water amplified his sense of drowning as he struggled to breathe.

"That's what you said a week ago. You've gambled away even more since then, and Urk don't run a charity. He said to collect one way or the other. And since you don't have the credits," the thug smiled as he drew an ugly black cylinder from a pocket, "today, it's the other."

Nick staggered as the neural whip lashed his chest, then screamed as the thug brought it back across his face. The whip's electronic thongs left black stripes across his red skin. One curled around the short, sensitive horns on his forehead, lifting him to his toes in agony. Whimpering, he fell to his knees. A rush of relief flooded his loins as Durkin swung the whip back for another blow, only to catch his partner Dweeble in the head instead.

"Ow! Ow, ow, ow! Watch what you're doing, you farking moron!" Holding his scorched forehead, Dweeble gave Durkin a hearty shove.

"Watch it yourself, Dweeble!" Durkin recovered his balance and grabbed his partner by the lapels.

Seeing his chance, Nick crawled away, then sprung to his feet and ran. As he turned a corner, he heard the smack of fists on flesh.

Nick kept going as he splashed down narrow alleys between run-down buildings of brown brick. Etched by eons of the planet Downside's nauseous climate, they loomed over him as he ran.

The mist soon turned into a frigid downpour, and he pulled up the hood of his jacket to ward it off. All that did was concentrate Downside's pervasive smell of rotting vegetation. As he slogged through the fetid mud, Nick thought this was one of the vilest planets he'd ever visited, and he couldn't wait till his ship reached for space.

Not that he needed more incentive to leave the place.

His next paycheck wouldn't cover what he owed to Urk, and everybody knew what happened to people who failed to pay their debts. It was hard to think that anything could be worse than a beating from a neural whip, but people disappeared without explanation, and the local organ banks never seemed short of material.

Nick hesitated at a street corner. Left would take him to the short-lease apartment he was using while his ship, the Vagabond, was in port for overhaul; right would take him to the spaceport. His shift didn't start until evening, but it would be an excellent place to hide from Urk's debt collectors for a bit. Security was tight, and even though his crew space was tiny, there was no way for Durkin or any other thugs to get to him. He could swing by his apartment later to get the set of grav tools he used to operate the ship's wormhole and the few other belongings he kept there.

Without conscious thought, Nick reached into his pocket for his lucky dice. Running them through his fingers helped him calm down while considering his options. Making up his mind, he turned right. A block later, he was on a main boulevard where he could catch a slidewalk to his destination.

When he reached the spaceport's gate, he tapped his thumb against the ID scanner. It compared his thumbprint with the personal ID chip embedded under his fingernail, verifying his identity. Then, after checking his access permissions with the AI that ran the port, it opened the gate. Nick scampered in, looking back to see if he had been followed. Though his spaceship was secure, the port itself was not. There was no knowing if Durkin or one of Urk's other goons had bribed their way in and might already be lurking there.

A few minutes later, he was at the Vagabond, where one of the ship's security guards was stationed at the crew hatch. Nick had heard that the captain was nervous about a prolonged stay in the refuse heap that passed for Downside's spaceport.

But when Nick tried to board, the guard stopped him and said, "I've been waiting for you. Got orders to take you right to the first mate."

"Why?"

The guard sneered and took him by the arm. "You'll find out soon enough."

He shoved Nick into the first mate's office a minute later. The first mate, a potato-shaped creature with multiple tentacles and myriad eyes, sat behind a polished aluminum desk. Glancing around, Nick felt his heartbeat speed up when he saw the chief engineer sitting in the corner of the room.

The chief engineer disliked ghoulies, a sentiment shared by most galactics, and had made Nick's employment miserable, blaming him for everything that went wrong. The satisfied look on the chief's space-pocked ochre face looked sinister.

"What's up?" Nick asked, trying to stay calm.

The first mate waved one of his tentacles, dismissing a holo display he had been scanning. Then, leaning forward, he fixed three of his five eyes on Nick and said, "I have a report indicating serious misconduct on your part."

"What, uh, would that be?" Nick fidgeted under the officer's withering glare and kept glancing at the chief, who remained silent.

"A surprise inventory has revealed that some expensive supplies are missing. Four cases of bivalve oil. At a thousand credits apiece, that's quite a sum. Of course, you wouldn't know anything about that, would you?"

"No! Of course not!"

"Yet, the video logs show that you are the only person who accessed the supplies locker when the items went missing."

"But I'm innocent. How can that be? I didn't—"

"Please, don't bother denying the facts. The chief engineer himself provided the logs to me. And your gambling problem is well-known. According to the chief, you're heavily in debt, and it's obvious you stole the supplies to pay it off."

Nick turned to stare at the chief, realizing he'd been set up.

Leaning back in his chair, the first mate continued, "Under the circumstances, I have no choice but to terminate your employment immediately and with prejudice. The cost of the missing supplies has been deducted from your final paycheck. And since the result is a negative number, no credits will be issued."

"But…but don't I get a hearing?"

"Yes. This was it." The first mate gestured to the waiting guard. "Throw this thief off the ship. And don't be gentle."

Before Nick could protest, the guard put him in a painful arm lock and frog-marched him out of the room. Another guard joined them in the hallway, grabbing Nick by the neck and his other arm.

When they reached the exit, the first guard smacked Nick in the head, making his eyes water as the world spun. The other guard kneed him in the hip, then together, they rushed Nick down the gangway and face-planted him in the mud.

For several moments, all Nick could do was lie in the soup and sob.

His dream of becoming rich and respected seemed farther away than ever. Not only was he deep in debt to a notoriously blood-thirsty loan shark, but now he'd lost his job. And was stuck on Downside. The prospect of being stranded on a planet whose chief export was pessimism left Nick deeply depressed.

Gathering himself, Nick got to his feet, pausing for a moment until the world stopped spinning. Then, rubbing his left shoulder, he limped away from the spaceport. Stunned at his savage turn of bad luck, Nick tried to think of where to go where he might be safe. Nothing came to mind. Hopping on the slidewalk, he headed into town, vaguely intending to return to his apartment.

2

As he rode the slidewalk from the planet's lone spaceport into the surrounding slums, Nick's shoulders slumped, and he wiped the rain from his eyes. He sneezed as Downside's predominant fragrance attacked his sinuses. Wet, cold, and broke, he was running out of options. The daily downpour just emphasized an outlook that made the expression 'down on your luck' sound encouraging.

The credit chip under his fingernail still had a meager amount of funds left, which he thought he could make last another day or two if careful. But the solace of a cold draft of Glurb ale was seductively appealing, and he needed something to pick up his spirits. So when Nick saw the Blue Sky Bar & Grill's flashing sign, he left the slidewalk and slipped into his favorite dive.

He smiled at the sweet smell of sizzling glorpburger that the bar's owners piped in from a vent over the door, then wrinkled his nose as the planet's default aroma overwhelmed it. The bar had the damp, musty reek characteristic of every building on Downside.

Nick lingered under the doorway's auto-dryer for a bit longer than usual. There was no way he could afford a private de-dampening pod, and this would surely be the last free thing the Blue Sky would offer him.

A dozen tables to Nick's left were populated by aliens from many worlds in various states of intoxication. It was hard to tell if a couple of pallid worm-like beings from Catpil VII had fallen down drunk or were just making their ponderous way to the refresher booth.

The heavy thump of a hypnotic techno-beat punctuated by the crystal dissonance of Kintaran chimes blared from an overhead music streamer. Half a dozen folk wobbled and twitched to the beat on a dance floor to the right while a small group of grasshopper-like jikli cracked out on Koke twirled on the iridescent ceiling.

The Blue Sky's horseshoe-shaped bar of polished oogerwood bulged into the center of the room like an onramp to paradise. Nick headed straight for it, then paused when he saw who was sitting there. It was Egrog, an amorphous being from the planet Gob. Currently in the form of a sphere, the gobbet was bright turquoise, indicating it was in a relaxed, happy mood.

Before Nick could turn around, the gobbet extruded a dozen tentacles with eyeballs, all focused on him.

"Nicky! Just the guy I was looking for!"

"Uh, hi, Egrog. What brings you to these parts?"

Nick's hesitation came from recent, painful experience. The gobbet was a grifter to the core of his narcissistic soul and could no more resist the opportunity to swindle another being than a child could set aside a favorite candy.

In contrast, Nick had the pragmatic attitude common to other ghoulies that, coupled with an ineradicable naivety, a tendency toward situational ethics, and a weakness for games of chance, left him easy prey for Egrog's get-rich-quick schemes.

"Nicky, I was hoping we could have a drink and chat about a little project I've got going."

"Ah, well, now's not the best time—"

"Nonsense! Any time is a good time to have a drink with my favorite ghoulie."

"I'm the only ghoulie you know, Egrog, so that's not quite a compliment."

"Hey, you're not still mad about that little mix-up on Frangaline II?"

Nick sighed, then took a seat next to the roughly spherical creature. "I guess not."

"Of course not! It's not like I meant to leave you there. And the locals let you off with just a warning, right? No blood, no foul, as they say on Earth?"

"Not familiar with the saying." Nick's unease grew as he looked at his occasional partner. "You haven't been hanging out with some earthlings, have you? You're the last person I'd expect to get religion."

Egrog laughed. Earth had two exports of interest to galactic civilization, one of which was the soft-drink Koke, which proved to be a highly addictive and pleasant stimulant for many species. The other was missionaries. Most worlds barely had the enthusiasm to produce one religion. Humans brought dozens with them when they ventured into space. Dismayed at the lack of spiritual engagement of galactic civilization, humanity responded with a vigorous stream of missionaries determined to bring salvation to every sentient being in the universe.

In Nick's experience, Earth's missionaries were generally welcomed by the various races of the galaxy. The more advanced civilizations viewed them with amusement, much as one might indulge a well-meaning but somewhat dim pet who insisted on bringing you your slippers in the morning even if you were already shod. On the other hand, civilizations still reaching for space took full advantage of the missionaries' technical and monetary resources in exchange for just a few minutes a week of prayer. And, of course, there were a few less-evolved species who treated the arrival of a shipload of missionaries like the local food truck and sincerely appreciated the free meal.

"No, Nicky, I'm not the religious type."

Nick took a moment to scan the holo-menu floating over the bar. The lingering smell of roast glorpburger was irresistible, and he ordered one with a basket of wiffle-fries. The finger-sized fries were deep-fried and tended to be salty. So he added a mug of his favorite drink, Glurb ale, a beer enhanced with the more potent purple glurb.

"So, how come you're suddenly spouting Earth talk?"

Before answering, Egrog extruded a slender tentacle, formed it into a straw, and then took a sip from a schooner of straight purple glurb.

He sighed. "Nicky, you'd be surprised what you might learn hanging around with some humans. They send ships out to every quadrant of the galaxy, and some of those who come back have stories that would curl your antennae."

"I like my antennae just the way they are," Nick said, shifting uneasily on his stool. Ghoulies had long, feathery antennae that they kept hidden in the short horns that projected from their forehead. Their antennae were sensitive organs, and he considered it rude to mention them unless you were a close friend or family member. At the moment, Nick didn't think Egrog qualified on either account.

"Of course you do, didn't mean to offend!"

Egrog extended a tentacle and patted Nick on the back. "So, how come you're hanging at the Blue Sky at this time of day? I thought you had the evening shift on the Vagabond. Are you just stopping in for a cold one before work, or did the boss give you shore leave for bad behavior?"

Egrog chuckled at his own joke, then stopped when Nick scowled at him.

"Egrog, I just lost my job, and I'm deep in debt to Urk. Durkin and one of his buddies beat me up this morning and said I'd get worse if I missed another payment. And we both know what that means." Nick looked around nervously before continuing. "But the Vagabond's first mate won't give me my last paycheck because of disciplinary termination. Not a good time for any of your jokes."

"Hey, sorry, I didn't realize that. What happened at work? Why'd they let you go?"

"When I showed up for my shift, the chief engineer accused me of stealing some bivalve lube."

"Did you?"

"No. But the company's accountants ran a surprise inventory check when we docked two weeks ago, and they must have found some missing."

"Do you know who did it? Maybe turn him in and get your job back?"

"Ha! I'm sure it was the chief engineer himself, but I've got no proof. Besides, they looked up my record on rGov and noted what happened on Frangaline II. Bastoviches didn't even give me two weeks' severance."

"Ouch!"

"Yeah. I tried to complain, but the security guards grabbed me and just tossed me out the hatch like I was day-old flurb meat. They wouldn't have treated me like that if I was a kintaran or flufflpertan, but ghoulies just don't get any respect. It's discrimination, I tell you!"

"Chill, dude! Don't get your antennae in a twad!"

"That's easy for you to say, Egrog. You can take any form you want. And by the way, keep your pseudopod out of the fries! You've already eaten half the basket, and I'm short on credit."

"No problem, Nicky!" Egrog withdrew his offending body part, snatching a fistful of fries as he did. "And a smart guy like you shouldn't have to worry about money. Which is what I wanted to talk with you about. If you're interested, it could mean the score of a lifetime. You'd never have to worry about credits again."

"Egrog, I didn't make a single credit on the last caper you pulled me into and nearly ended up in a recivilization center. If I could get a real job on another starship, I could pay Urk back enough to keep from another beating. Or worse. But in this economy? Do you know how many ships' crews got laid off when the market for purple glurb tanked due to short supplies?

Who knew the interstellar economy would be impacted by something like that? And it's not like my training as a wormhole engineer translates to a job on the ground. rGov won't even let us run simulations inside a planet's gravity well, let alone crack open a portal to another world."

Egrog shifted his bulk, oozing into a somewhat upright pillar on his bar stool, before replying, "Well, what did you expect? After that idiot on Reamus II opened a wormhole to a gas giant that sucked in half a continent before they could close it, people have been a little touchy about that sort of thing. Only the big commercial starliners and government starships are trusted to operate portable wormhole generators. It takes longer for the rest of us to travel to a local wormgate, but it's safer than unregulated wormholes."

"Yeah, I get that. The worst part is ghoulies aren't very popular anyway, and when ladies find out what I do for a living, they find somebody else to talk to. Know how long it's been since I had a date?"

"Sorry to hear that, Nicky. You'd never have trouble picking up chicks if you were a gobbet like me." Egrog briefly formed a tentacle into something large and obscene, then hastily reabsorbed it as a tall, green mantid approached.

"I saw that," she said, scootching up to the bar next to Egrog. "My name's Alice. I've heard stories about you gobbets. Didn't know they were true."

Egrog went from his usual shade of turquoise to a squalid magenta, something Nick recognized as indicating a state of internal distress. He hid a smile at his friend's predicament. The gobbet's piratical sex life had just hit a shoal. The females from Mantis were known across the galaxy for their ferocious creativity when mating, which often left a male crippled and occasionally missing his head. What one might do with a being that could take any shape was one of those questions best pondered over a punch bowl spiked with purple glurb at fraternity mixers among the less prestigious universities.

Mantids were also notoriously warlike, forming the backbone of rGov's heavy infantry, and Nick edged back a bit at the sight of three diagonal lavender stripes on Alice's green thorax, indicating that she was a platoon leader. Several icons below them showed that though young, she had already fought in multiple campaigns.

And though her face was covered with inflexible chitin, she had large, expressive eyes with long curly lashes, and Nick could see that she was looking for adventure, hopefully in all the wrong places. Egrog withdrew all of his appendages, leaving just a single eyestalk poking out of his body, which had shifted to a dingy yellow.

"Well, you shouldn't believe everything you hear. We're not that different from other folks, and we've got feelings. Not everybody appreciates how sensitive we are."

"Of course, sweetie. If it gets you in the mood, I'll light up a candle while you light me up with your, er, special abilities."

"I'm sorry, but I'm not interested, Alice."

"Ooh, I love how you trill the 'I' when you say my name. It's so sexy!"

"Seriously, I'm not—"

"Oh, of course you are. I've seen you in here before and watched you pick up fawning, swag-bellied drabs like the ones at that table over there. You're no monk."

"Look, uh…"

"Alice. My name's Alice."

"Yes, well Alice, I'm just not sure we're really compatible, you know?"

Alice sidled closer, cuddling up to Egrog, then slowly ran her hand down his back. Or what passed for a back on a gobbet, lightly touching his skin with the razor-sharp tips of her nails. "Oh, we're compatible. And I can do things for you those other girls can't."

She leaned close and whispered something Nick couldn't make out, running her hand down Egrog's body again. The gobbet turned magenta where she touched him, leaving a vivid streak that contrasted nicely with the dull yellow of the rest of his body.

"Looks like you've got your hands, that is, pseudopods full, buddy." Nick tapped the credit chip located under his fingernail on the counter to pay for his meal. "I'm outta here. You lovebirds have fun."

Alice slid even closer to Egrog as he wailed, "Wait! Nicky, don't leave me like this!"

Nick paused, one eyebrow lifted in sardonic amusement.

"Nicky, I got a deal for you. Can get you out of your current jam if you're interested."

Nick hesitated. "Whatcha got in mind?"

Egrog protruded a half dozen tentacles with eyes and scanned the room, overlooking Alice's sudden focus on their conversation. "Can't talk here. But it's a real score, could set us both up for life."

"Why me?"

"As I was just saying, you have certain talents that are currently, ahem, going wasted. I can put them to good use."

Nick scowled, "No thanks, bud. I barely stayed out of jail after your last scheme fell through. Not interested in another one."

"I'd be interested in anything you might have in mind," Alice purred, stroking the gobbet again.

"But, Nicky," Egrog protested, "I need your help on this one. Really. Truly."

"Enough! Talk to you later."

As Nick left the bar, he chuckled at the sight of his friend trying to extricate himself from the mantid's attentions.

3

Outside the Blue Sky Bar & Grill, a light, gray rain was falling, which constituted a fine day on Downside. Nick's worn boots made light pishing sounds as he walked to the tram stop at the end of the block. To his dismay, he got an "insufficient credit" message when he tapped his finger chip on the tram's kiosk. He'd thought he still had enough credit left for a few essentials, but the Blue Sky had taken more than he could afford.

With a sigh, he turned up the hood on his faded black windbreaker and began the long trudge back to his apartment.

Nick's walk home took longer than usual. The area around the Blue Sky, a typical spaceport dive bar, was seedy, but the neighborhood where Nick parked his bones at night was the kind of place that aspired to be a slum. Its chief attraction was that the hotels and apartments in the area were cheap and available for hourly rentals. Other than down-on-their-luck spacers, it was populated by a full complement of the junkies, thieves, and cutthroats who normally tenanted such places.

Avoiding contact with those folk or any of Urk's people who might be looking for him involved a couple of detours and one brief stint hiding under the cracked foundation of a brothel. Nick's relief upon reaching his apartment faded when the door failed to open.

Nick tapped his chip finger on the manual entry panel, wondering if the door's auto-scan system had failed again and could not identify him via its biometric sensors. A message appeared on the door when he did:

"Greetings, valued client!

"Your rent is now two days overdue. Due to an insufficiency of funds in your credit chip, you are now locked out of your apartment. All of your possessions will be sold at auction in three days, giving you a chance to recover anything of sentimental value. Please plan to pay in cash.

"Thank you for staying at the Rigellian Arms Apartments. Have a nice day!"

Nick stared at the message in dismay. A pang of regret at having spent too much at the Blue Sky shouted down his tummy's happy gurgling as it digested the glorpburger. He'd known his credit was low and that he shouldn't have indulged. He was reduced to living on the street if he couldn't cover staying in a hovel like the Arms. In the rain.

Sliding down, he sat on the floor with his back to the door and considered his options. There were precisely two:

He could go outside and wait for one of the local thugs to cut his throat.

Or, he could find some spectacularly effective way to make a large sum of money overnight. The only idea he had along those lines was to call Egrog and find out his latest scam.

Option number one had a certain lack of style, and Nick felt a personal aversion to death in most—if not all—of its forms. But it was still probably better than the alternative. Egrog's schemes did seem to keep the gobbet flush with credit, but little of the wealth ever seemed to attach itself to his partners, something Nick had personally experienced several times.

Sudden shouting outside caught Nick's attention. Not that loud voices were uncommon in the neighborhood, but the fact that the shouting ended with the rippling harmonic chime of a molecular disrupter was concerning. Only heavies in the employ of the loan-shark Urk could afford that kind of weaponry. And Nick had an outstanding debt of sufficient size to incent said individual to dispatch his minions to recover either funds or blood.

Even one of Egrog's schemes was starting to sound attractive.

As Nick slipped out a basement window of the Arms, he took a quick peek at the building's entrance. As feared, Durkin was there with a couple of Urk's other enforcers, and there was no mistaking the disrupters in their hands. Or the shredded body at their feet. Straining his ears, he could just hear them talking.

"Dweeble, you idiot! We were supposed to bring the body back in good enough condition to harvest some of the organs. Reset your disruptor to stun mode for the next guy on our list."

"Sorry, boss. Who's next?"

"That ghoulie who got in over his head. Urk's seriously unhappy we let him get away earlier, so we better not mess this up. Jerk missed too many payments—"

Nick didn't wait to hear the rest, scuttling away as quietly and quickly as he could. While he did, he mentally composed a quick message to his friend, Egrog. The comm implant in his skull picked up the electrical signals corresponding to his words, translated them into Galactic Standard text, and squirted them across the Stellarnet to Egrog.

"Egrog, I've decided to ['Buy Bimyo knives – guaranteed ever sharp!'] join your caper. Where ['End embarrassing stains! Buy Kimoi sanitary pads!'] can we meet?"

Nick groaned as he scanned the outgoing message. The social media platform he used, Slymebook, had inserted advertisements between every couple of words. Being unable to pay for a premium account, Nick was reduced to using the free version, supported by extensive and intrusive marketing. The ads were rarely relevant, and Nick wasn't sure what value there was in promoting adult diapers to somebody like Egrog, but it was all he could afford.

Egrog's response came while Nick hid under the vinyl skirt of a parked hovercraft. Interrupted by frequent ads, it streamed like a ticker-tape across Nick's retinal implant.

"Super! You won't ['Buy Oodles for your doodles!'] regret this. Meet me ['Free! Vacation in scenic Grosspit!'] outside the Blue Sky in half an hour. ['Time is money! Save both at the bank of Nertl!']"

Nick scanned his surroundings before slipping out from under the hovercraft. A quick dart down a dark alley and then a dash up a narrow street led him back to the city's main thoroughfare. Nick kept looking back to see if any of Urk's goons were following him but couldn't see any. He figured they'd be less likely to gun him down in the middle of a crowded street, but it was better to be careful than demolecularized.

A block from the Blue Sky, he stopped at the entrance to a clothing store. Standing in the alcove, he pretended to examine the latest fashion in low-cost raincoats while watching for either Egrog or Urk's goons.

Hands in his pockets, Nick nervously rattled his lucky dice.

"Meep! Meep, meep!"

Looking down, Nick saw a small, brightly colored bird huddled on the ground next to him. Crouching, he said, "Hey, little purtybird. What's a fancy guy like you doing on this planet?"

"Meep!"

"Where's your owner? Rich folk don't normally let their expensive pets run loose. And you look like you've been out here a while."

"Meep! Chitty-chitty meep, meep!"

Nick picked up the semi-sentient creature in his palm, cupping his other hand over it to protect it from the drizzle. Purtybirds came from a tropical, sun-drenched planet, and it was sad to see one in such a bedraggled state. Having just been evicted from his apartment, he could empathize with another creature who also seemed homeless.

"I can feel you shivering. You must be cold." Nick unzipped his jacket and held the bird inside to warm it.

With a sigh, he pulled a wiffle-fry out of a pocket. It was somewhat the worse for wear, given his latest efforts to avoid involuntary commitment to an organ bank. Roughly the size of his middle finger, the fry drooped from the humidity, and one end had broken off.

"I was saving this for a snack later. I'm broke, and it's all I've got to eat unless Egrog comes up with something quick. But you look like you need it more than I do."

The bird snatched the fry from Nick's hand as soon as he offered it. Gulping it down in three quick bites, it gave a chortling chirp, nipped Nick's finger so hard it drew blood, and then flew off, lightening the load as it went.

"That's what I get for being a nice guy," Nick muttered. Wiping his hand against the store's wall, he zipped his coat against the rain and settled back to wait for Egrog.

An uncomfortable period passed, and Nick was about to leave when he felt a tap on his shoulder. Startled, he looked to see who it was but saw only a thin gray tentacle hanging down from the roof. It formed a finger and pointed up, then disappeared from sight.

Nick sighed, then entered the shop. When the clerk wasn't looking, he slipped into the back room, where he found a flight of stairs leading to the rooftop.

It took him a minute to locate his friend on the roof. Egrog had changed into a shade of gray that matched the rain and then flattened himself along a low wall that circled the roof.

"Is it all clear?" Egrog asked in a low whisper.

Nick looked around, then crouched next to his friend. "Yeah, I think I shook off Urk's boys on the way here."

"Urk's still after you?"

"Yeah. That's what you were worried about, wasn't it?" Nick waved his hand as he spoke to ward off a swarm of midges. The bugs had evolved the ability to swim and fly simultaneously through Downside's damp atmosphere. One bit Nick on the cheek before he could pull the hood of his rain jacket tighter for protection.

"No. It's that mantid, Alice. She's got the hots for me, and I'd just as soon not get involved."

Nick chuckled. "I thought it was something serious."

"It is, man! You know what they say about mantid mating habits. I'd rather not lose my head!"

"Well, I think you're safe there—you don't have a head! Anyway, there were only a couple of jikli in the shop when I came up."

"Good! Now then, let's talk about getting you back in the money."

"I'm listening."

"Ever heard of a place called Altimus?"

"Yeah, everybody's heard that legend. The people on that planet held the secret of eternal life. But its location was lost three thousand solar cycles ago during the last uprising on the planet Grunt, and nobody's been able to find it since. The way I heard it, the folks on Altimus didn't want to share their secret with the grunts. The grunts didn't take that so well and blasted the planet into microscopic dust particles."

"Yeah, that's the official story. But Nicky, my lad, what if Altimus hadn't been destroyed? If it was still out there?"

"Seems iffy to me. Why?"

"Well, wouldn't you like to be rich and live forever?"

Nick looked around at the squalid, rain-drenched spaceport. "Here?"

"No, you fool! Not on this wretched planet. Someplace nice, like Kintares III."

"Well, that would be nice, but I don't have any way to get there, and even if I did, I couldn't afford to stay."

"Nicky, my lad, what I've got in mind will take care of all that!"

"How?"

"I know where Altimus is."

Nick snorted in derision, an act his overloaded mucus membranes made somewhat gross.

"Okay, I don't know personally. But I know somebody who does and who's willing to help."

"Really? Who?"

"An earthling missionary that I bumped into a few weeks ago. I'll introduce you if you're in, and she can fill you in herself."

Nick thought about that for a few minutes.

"Okay, but if this is another of your—"

"You won't regret this! I promise!" Egrog patted Nick on the back with a couple of tentacles. "Hang on while I send a quick message…there we go. Yep, she'll be up in a minute."

Several minutes passed while they waited for Egrog's missionary to appear. The rain picked up during the interval, and Nick pulled his jacket tight around his neck in a futile effort to stay dry. He could feel trickles of water running down his back and was unsure whether his wet socks resulted from top-down leakage or bottom-up seepage.

Then a figure appeared at the top of the stairs.

The earthling was a head taller than Nick and of robust dimensions. Clearly female and mammalian, her heavy torso plowed through the downpour like the prow of an ocean liner. Under her green rain slicker, Nick could see that she had a small nose set in a round head. Her blue eyes had the suspicious expression of someone who discovered too early that most adults had the reasoning capacity of salt-water taffy.

"Nicky, meet Mindy," Egrog said with a flourish. "Mindy, meet my best bud, Nicky."

"My pleasure," Mindy said, holding her hand out as she brushed aside strands of long brown hair that had escaped her rain hood and blown into her mouth.

"Likewise." Nick stared at the hand, puzzled. At a nudge from Egrog, he asked, "Is there something you want me to do with your hand?"

Mindy laughed. "Yeah, Earth people shake hands when they meet."

"Why?"

"To show we're friendly."

Nick furrowed his brow in concentration. "Why would you do that? Doesn't that give things away if you need to negotiate with somebody? Don't people take advantage of you when you do that?"

Mindy stared at him for a moment, then lowered her hand. "Not really. But I guess a demon wouldn't understand."

"How do you mean that?" Nick tilted his head to the side as he returned Mindy's stare.

"Hold on, folks! We're all friends here!" Egrog put his tentacles around their shoulders, a gesture that lost some effect due to the water dripping from the pseudopods.

"Mindy, I was just bringing Nicky here up to speed on our little project. How about you fill him in with what you learned about Altimus when you were on Grunt?"

Mindy sniffed, then nodded. "Okay. You want the full story or just the highlights?"

Nick folded his arms, not sure what to make of the earthling. And he was curious what a planet like Grunt with a worse reputation than Downside might have to do with getting rich. "Just the highlights, and if you can explain how I come into this, that would be appreciated."

"Fine. Here's how it happened.

"About twenty cycles ago, when I was a teenager, my parents booked the family onto a mission flight to the planet Grunt."

"Grunt?"

"Yeah, Grunt. We'd been trying for centuries to get a team on that benighted world to bring them the word of God. We finally got a break when one of the missionary techs was able to hack into rGov's security system. He got the planet's location and the bypass codes for the force field enclosing the planet.

Nick scowled. "So, you were a missionary?"

"Yeah. Why, you got a problem with that?"

"My Aunt Baleface was religious, like most folk on Ghoul."

"So?"

"I got a beating and a lecture on my evil ways every time I did something wrong. It got worse when she caught me gambling. I never fit in there, so I left Ghoul as soon as I got my grav tech license. I've avoided religious people ever since."

Mindy returned his scowl. "Well, you're safe with me. I quit that life, and I'm not going back.

Mindy tilted her head to the side and gave Nick a considering look. "I have to say, you're not what I expected. I thought grav techs made good money; you look like a bum."

Turning to Egrog, she asked, "Are you sure this guy's going to be able to help us?"

Egrog colored bright pink. "Yes, Mindy, he's the best grav tech this side of Kintares. Just down on his luck at the moment."

Mindy gave Nick a calculating look. "How'd that happen? And why would you want to help us?"

Nick felt his face flush hot with embarrassment. He'd hoped his personal problems wouldn't come out, but it seemed there was no avoiding it. "I lost a lot of credit at the tables, and I owe Urk a…a lot."

"Who's Urk?"

"Nasty loan shark," Egrog volunteered.

"So if he comes along, we're borrowing trouble, aren't we?"

Egrog went red with anger. "Mindy, I asked you to trust me on this. Nick's never let me down. And once we're off planet, we won't have to worry about Urk."

Mindy stared at Nick for a long time before saying, "Does he know what he's getting into?"

"Not entirely," Egrog said diffidently.

"I see. Well, to get back to the story, those codes change weekly, so there wasn't time to put together a properly equipped and organized mission. So our bishop grabbed as many missionary families as possible, which was about a hundred, and stuffed us onto a mission ship.

"We hit Grunt three days later, and at first, everything went according to plan. We slipped past the force field without a problem and landed on an abandoned field at their largest spaceport. It was deserted, which we expected, given that they hadn't been allowed into space for centuries.

"We didn't see anybody for several days, so teams explored the spaceport. Our leaders finally made contact with the locals, and we were invited to a welcome feast the next day. My uncle must have seen or heard something that worried him on the way there because he suddenly said he was sick and had to return to the ship. He asked my parents to send my little brother and me along to help him get back. I didn't think anything of it until we were out of sight of the group, then he grabbed us and ran like the devil back to the ship."

"How does a devil run?" Nick asked, his curiosity piqued.

"You should know. You look like one."

"How do you mean? Wait a sec! Are you saying—"

"Nothing, she isn't saying anything, are you Mindy?" Egrog glared at the woman with half a dozen eyeballs.

"Guess not. Anyway, when we got back to the ship, Uncle Joe locked it up and changed the access codes. I thought that was pretty weird until our leader reappeared with a dozen grunts an hour later. He tried to get in, then tried to make my uncle let him in, but Uncle Joe refused. I didn't understand why, and Uncle Joe said it smelled wrong. He turned out to be right. When the grunts saw we weren't letting them on the ship, they disemboweled our leader and ate him. Raw.

"After that, Uncle Joe called rGov security for assistance. They showed up a few hours later, but it was too late to help anybody. The grunts had cooked and eaten the entire mission-ary team by then.

"The rGov agents dropped a few bombs on the locals to break up the feast, but I could tell their hearts weren't in it, and they hauled us outta there without doing anything significant.

"After that, I dropped out of missionary life. I was working as a travel agent at the Downside airport when I bumped into Egrog. And here we are."

Nick looked at Egrog, then at Mindy. "Nice story. Sorry about your folks. I really am. But what's this got to do with me? Or this plan to make a fortune overnight?"

Egrog quickly responded, "Ah, that's the key part of Mindy's story, isn't it? Mindy, tell Nicky what you saw when exploring the spaceport."

"Oh, yeah. I still get kinda shook up when I think about what happened. So, when we were exploring the spaceport, we found a vast building twice the size of anything near it. Inside, it was filled with artifacts from all the worlds the grunts had visited, and we figured out pretty quick that it was their Temple of Conquest.

"Each of the displays, and there were quite a few, had a star map hung on the wall above it."

Mindy stopped there, and Nick looked back and forth between Egrog and Mindy, waiting for more. When there wasn't, he asked, "So, I still don't see how this has anything to do with me. Mind explaining?"

"Oh, that." Egrog colored light blue, the gobbet equivalent to a sheepish grin. "You see, the Temple of Conquest has a star map showing every planet the grunts looted. And we know that they hit Altimus hard. So there must be a map to Altimus somewhere in that building."

Nick suddenly felt the kind of stomach spasm he usually associated with eating spoiled chitin chips with his whiffle burger. "And you need me because?"

"Without the access codes for the force field, the only way to get to Grunt is to open a wormhole directly to the planet. And you're the best I know."

"Are you crazy! You know what rGov does to anybody who even thinks about doing that!"

"Cool down, Nicky, it's not as dangerous as you think. We don't need a full-size wormhole to fly a ship through. Just a keyhole, large enough for the three of us to slip through."

"You mean the four of us, don't you, sweetie?"

Egrog jumped in surprise, then curled up into a tight, magenta ball with only a single eyestalk exposed. "Alice! What are you doing here? And how did you get up here without me seeing you?"

As she approached, the mantid flexed her hands, revealing a set of impressive talons she usually kept retracted. "Climbed the wall, Yummykins. One of my many special abilities. Come to my place sometime, and I'll show you more."

"Er, no thanks, Alice. Can't. Busy."

"Oh yes, busy with your little trip to Grunt. A highly illegal stunt."

"What we do is none of your business."

"True, but rGov will be very interested."

"You wouldn't!"

"Wouldn't I? Well, maybe if you were a little nicer to me instead of treating me like a gleeking, toad-spotted mammet, I might have second thoughts. And, of course, if you let me come along, then my silence would be guaranteed."

"That's extortion!"

Alice tapped Egrog's trembling bulk with the tip of a claw. "Of course it is, dear. All's fair, as they say."

"Who says that?" Nick asked, puzzled by the expression.

"Never mind," Mindy said. "I'll explain it to you later. Right now, we've got to make a decision. And Egrog, it looks like you'll have to take one for the team."

"Take one of what?" Nick asked, even more puzzled.

Egrog sighed. "Never mind, Nicky. It just means we've got a new team member. Welcome aboard, Alice."

"Delighted!" she exclaimed, settling down next to Egrog. "So, when do we leave?"

"Just as soon as Nicky collects his tools. I reserved a compartment on a tramp shuttle up to the system's main gateway. Once we're there, Nicky can use the gateway's maintenance system to open a keyhole to Grunt."

"Wait a sec! I never said I'd do this." Nick folded his arms. He felt Mindy was holding something back, and the whole proposition gave him the willies.

"Well, what other options have you got?"

Nick sighed as his shoulders sagged in defeat. "None, but you haven't mentioned how we split the grift if this all works. And then there's the small problem of getting my tools out of my apartment. Or did you forget the part of my text where I said I was locked out?"

"The split's equal shares for all survivors."

"Survivors?" Nick muttered with a frown.

"As for your tool kit, it shouldn't be too hard to crack the security system of a dump like the Rigellian Arms." Egrog extruded several hair-thin tentacles. "Never met a lock I couldn't pick."

Whatever Egrog's reservations about Alice might be, Nick appreciated that she had sufficient funds to rent an aircab to take them to his apartment. It took only a moment to enter their destination and payment into the cab's nav unit. The autopilot engaged and launched the cab into the air as soon as the door closed. While they floated above the ocher roofs of the city, Egrog formulated a plan to liberate Nick's belongings.

"Your apartment's on the second floor, right?"

"Yeah."

"And it's got a window?"

"Yeah."

"Then this'll be easier than taking burble treats from a dumbird. Drop me on the roof when we fly over. I'll let down a tentacle to the window, ooze my way inside, then unlock the door for the rest of you."

"What if Urk's goons show up?"

"Why would they, now that you're locked out?"

Nick frowned. "How would they know that?"

"Dummy!" Egrog tapped Nick on the forehead with a tentacle. "Urk's a silent partner in most of the businesses around here. You can bet your aunt Baleful Glance that he knows. Besides, why would he send goons around to harvest your internal organs if he thought there was a chance you could still make your payments?"

"But I have a LieLock personal firewall! How can he get through that to see what my finances are?"

"Dude, you're broke. Have you checked that your firewall is still up?"

"What?" Nick concentrated his thoughts, and his LieLock dashboard appeared on his retina. The message "Deactivated Due to Insufficient Funds" was displayed.

"No! How can they do that?"

"You know how it goes, Nicky. No money, no honey. That's just the way things are. If you want to change them, then you need to get solvent. Quick. And my little plan is just what you need to do that."

"But rGov—"

"Doesn't have a clue. Mindy here's the only sentient to see the Temple of Conquest in eons, and they don't know that she saw it. She was on the missionary ship when rGov's rescue team picked her up."

Nick looked around, desperate for any other option. Mindy returned his glance with a silent stare; Alice extended a talon and used it to hone one of her mandibles, a process that gave off a treble screech that made Nick's toes clench, which was, of course, the purpose of the action. Mantids weren't known to be subtle.

As the aircab settled down over the roof of Nick's erstwhile apartment complex, Egrog cracked open a door and poured himself out onto the building's roof like a giant blob of orange honey. Once on the rooftop, he flattened out and extruded a tentacle down two floors to the window of Nick's apartment.

Mindy and Alice leaned out to watch while Egrog flowed around the window. Then, seeping in around the edges of the panel, he gave a sudden heave, and the glass flew away from the building to shatter on the ground below.

Egrog disappeared inside and, a moment later, stuck a tentacle out the window, waving for the rest of the team to join him.

While the aircab hovered outside his apartment window, Nick tentatively stepped across and joined Egrog inside.

"Grab your gear!" Egrog said. "It won't take long for Urk's goons to respond to our break-in."

Nick scampered around the drab efficiency apartment, kicking aside food wrappers and empty beer cans as he gathered his equipment. He put it in a light backpack and was adding some clothes when the door opened, and Urk's debt collectors strode into the room.

Nick's heart stuttered like a diesel engine running out of gas at the sight. Dweeble took up a position at the door, leveling a laser rifle at Egrog. Durkin grabbed Nick by the shirt and stuck the muzzle of a harmonic disrupter under his chin.

"Gotcha, you little squib!" he chortled, "time to pay up or check out."

"Uh, take it easy with that thing!" Nick said, dancing on his tiptoes in a vain attempt to put distance between his head and the gun. "I'll pay, honest, I will!"

"Sure. Like, right now."

"Hey, I just need a little more time."

"Urk says your time's up."

"But I just need a few days. I've got something in the works that'll pay out enough to cover my whole debt."

"Really? What?"

"I can't say."

"Oh yeah? Well, you better if you want to keep breathing."

"Seriously, I—"

"Enough gab! I'm gonna—"

Whatever Urk's man planned to do would forever remain a mystery. With his head forced back, Nick saw that, during the confrontation, Alice had slipped out of the aircab and stealthily picked her way across the ceiling. Holding firm with the claws of her back and middle legs, she reached down with her front legs and decapitated the thug with one efficient swipe of her talons.

Then she threw the head at the gunman waiting by the door. The head hit Dweeble's forehead with a solid smack, sending yellow goo flying everywhere. Stunned, the creature slumped to the floor. Alice dropped on top of him and reduced him to something resembling potatoes O'Brien with a few deft slashes.

Turning to Nick, she asked, "Got your stuff?"

"Yeah," Nick said softly, staring at the twitching corpses in horror. Then, looking down at the lemon-curd entrails splattered across his jacket, he turned, bent, and barfed in one fluid motion.

Alice sniffed disdain. "What's the matter? Never seen the insides of a Thurbian before? If you don't want your apartment decorated the same way with your own guts, you better get your sorry derriere outta here!"

"He's going, he's going!" Egrog shouted, rushing to his friend's aid. "Come on, Nicky. She's right. Urk's goons would've been live-streaming the hit on you, so he already knows what happened. We need to scoot before more of his enforcers show up."

Nick let himself be led to the aircab where Mindy was waiting. She took a handkerchief and dabbed at his jacket as he settled down. Looking down at his shoes, she said, "Ew! I don't think those are gonna come clean with a paper towel. Do you have another pair?"

"No."

"Well—"

"Hang on!" Egrog shouted, interrupting Mindy as he took manual control of the aircab and sent it into a sharp dive. "Urk's goons had backup, and they're right behind us!"

As the little cab plummeted toward the concrete, part of the Plexi canopy disappeared in a rainbow of dust particles accompanied by the chime of a disrupter bolt.

"They're shooting at us!" Mindy screamed, tumbling to the floor on top of Nick as Egrog swerved to the right.

Crushed under the earth woman's bulk, Nick freed his head in time to see Alice brace herself in the canopy's opening and point back toward their pursuers. The cab resonated, and for a few seconds, Nick thought it would shake itself apart.

"What the hell was that?" Egrog yelled.

"Subsonic phonon ring," she replied. "I always wear one when I go out on a date. A girl can't be too careful, you know. And I think you can ease off now, Egrog. Those whey-faced maggot-pies have been neutralized."

"Say what?" Nick sputtered as the cab leveled off.

"Neutralized. As in, no longer a threat."

"Holy Mother of God!" Mindy whispered, peeking backward at an umber cloud of dust that had recently been a high-performance aircar. "You did that?"

"Yeah. Good shot, eh?"

"I'd say so. Where did you learn that?"

"Yeah," Egrog said, pivoting several eyeballs to stare at Alice. "Where did you learn to shoot like that? And that ring is outlawed on thirty-five planets. How'd you get your talons on that?"

"Oh, sure, now you want to get to know me," Alice said, sulking back into her seat. "An hour ago, you didn't want me around. I'm a sensitive girl, you know, and I've got feelings."

"Sorry," Egrog muttered, "so how about you share a bit?"

Alice brightened. "Well, if you must know, I'm just here on leave with some brood mates. We're attached to the 132nd Wafflestomper Brigade and have spent the last five cycles on Basalt III. Nothing but bare rock as far as a mantid can see. Downside sounded like a nice break from that."

"It must've been pretty nasty if Downside sounded good," Nick gasped, finally extracting himself from underneath Mindy. "But I think I've heard of your group before. Weren't you part of the army that suppressed the uprising on Righteous I?"

"Yeah, we were there. What of it?" Alice fidgeted a bit, clearly not liking where the conversation was going.

"Oh my god," Mindy said. "I heard about that. People were talking about genocide charges afterward."

"Nothing was proven!" Alice snarled. "Our orders were to clear the city, and we did."

"But there was no city left when you were done!"

"Well, they didn't say HOW they wanted the city cleared. Back home, that's how we do business. If they wanted something different, they should have told us."

"Okay," Egrog said, "good to know, but right now, we have a bigger problem."

"What's that?" Nick asked.

"Urk. Remember him?"

"Oh, yeah, Urk."

"He's not gonna be happy with what just happened. I give it five, maybe ten minutes before more of his goons show up. But this time, he won't send in his bill collectors. They'll be combat-trained enforcers."

"What do we do?"

"We get out of Dodge," Mindy said.

"I thought we were on Downside," Nick muttered, confused.

Egrog sighed. "Nicky, lad, it's just an earthling saying that means we need to leave fast."

"Oh. Well, I wish you'd just say what you mean!"

"Sure, no problem. Now, we need to get off-planet sooner than I'd planned. But our shuttle reservation isn't until tomorrow night. Any suggestions?"

"We could go to the spaceport and shoot our way onto the next shuttle," Alice suggested, clicking her fore-talons together.

Egrog went purple. "Really? And when rGov sends in a peacekeeper squad with orders to shoot first?"

"We die gloriously!"

"I'd rather not die at all," Nick muttered.

"Me neither," Mindy added. "But what if we found a way to sneak onto the next ship out?"

"That'll never work," Alice said with a sniff. "Even on a hick planet like this where they can't afford proper security, we'll still need somebody with a spacer ID to get past the entrance gate. Or more credits than we've got to bribe our way through."

All eyes turned to Nick, not counting a few extra ones that Egrog extruded in his enthusiasm.

"Nicky, boy. You don't suppose that your ID is still valid, do you?"

Nick slid down in his seat, frantically looking from side to side like a trapped rabbit. "I don't know. It depends on whether my ex-boss sent the notice of termination to the spaceport admin. Even then, they might not cancel my ID if they thought there was a chance I'd get another job on a ship."

"Could you get us on a ship?"

"Not as crew, and even if we found one with open passenger berths, it wouldn't be cheap. Besides, won't rGov be looking for us after what we did at the apartment?"

"If I know Urk, rGov will never know about him losing a couple of his goons."

"But, what about cash?"

Egrog turned orange, indicating a mix of excitement and pleasure as he banked their aircab toward the spaceport. "We'll worry about that when we get there."

Even with Mindy's help, Nick hadn't finished cleaning the Dweebian innards off his clothes when Egrog parked the aircab at the spaceport's gate. The daily rain had lightened to a gentle mist, for which Nick was glad as he bolted from the aircab, still holding his nose against the acrid stench of vomit and intestines. At least the daily drizzle would rinse off the remaining offal—he hoped.

Nick's stomach knotted in distress when he tapped his finger chip on the gate's authentication pad and was greenlighted. He didn't want to go back and face more of Urk's goons, but he also didn't like Egrog's plan, which was sure to get them all arrested.

While the group milled about, Nick asked, "Now what?"

"Just hang on a sec," Egrog replied. "Okay, I just scanned the departure schedule on Slymebook, and there's a cargo ship lifting for the system's wormgate in about an hour. That's our ride out."

"A cargo ship?"

"Yeah, we'll sneak on board and stay hidden till it reaches the gate. Then you do your magic, Nicky boy, and we're on our way to Grunt."

"How will we—"

"Wait and see, Nicky, just wait and see."

Followed by the rest of the group, Egrog hopped onto a slidewalk that took them halfway across the port, then transited to another that took them to a flower-shaped array of docking pads, only one of which was occupied.

The ship looked like a three-hundred-meter-high tin can left in the rain so long that the hull had accomplished the impossible, devolving into a color even grayer than the original shade of the metal. A ground-level cargo hatch looked like a giant doodlebeast mouth being noodled by a pair of obsolete lifterbots shuffling crates from a truck into the hold.

"Stay behind me," Egrog said as he flattened into the shape of a bowl high enough to screen Mindy, the tallest of the team. Then he shifted color until he had a passable match for a state of suicidal depression, blending perfectly with the drizzle.

"Nice camo," Alice said, "but won't they spot us on infrared?"

"Nope, I can adjust my hue from the ultraviolet to the deep infrared. Just stay behind me, and the ship's security scanner won't see anything. By the way, everybody needs to turn off their personal comm links while we're on the ship; otherwise, the ship's security will detect us."

Once inside, Egrog led them to a lift that ran the ship's length.

"I love these old tin cans," he chortled. "They cut corners on everything to keep them cheap, including the AIs flying them. Most don't even have an organic crew, but they all have cabins just in case organics do cop a ride. Once I hack the AI, we'll have the ship to ourselves, and nobody will ever know we were here."

Being fully automated, the ship didn't have a bridge. Instead, a multipurpose room in the ship's middle contained a small control console and a Tummyrot food synthesizer.

Egrog led the team into the room, then squatted in front of a control console.

"Standard design," He said, "This'll only take a moment."

With a bright "ching," the unit produced three bowls of lumpy treacle.

"Are you sure that's the control console, not the food synth?" Mindy asked.

"Sorry," he said, dark purple with embarrassment. "They must've changed the design on these things since I last hitched a ride on one."

While he poked his tendrils into the other console to hack the system, Alice dipped a mandible into a soup bowl.

"Just like the Pigalian soup they serve us back in the barracks," she said, digging in.

Mindy sniffed at it and made a face. "If that's what you had to eat on campaign, I can understand the homicidal rage when you attacked the Righteous I congregation. I'm hungry, but there's no way I'm eating this slop. Egrog, can't you do any better?"

Nick squeezed in next to Egrog. "Here, I'll do it. They had these on the last couple of ships I worked on. You just have to know how they work."

Seventeen bowls of Pigalian soup later, Nick gave up. "It must be broke," he muttered, avoiding the stares of his friends.

Egrog oozed away from the control console and said, "I can't stomach that glop either. You're a master technician, Nicky. I'm sure you can fix it if you try. While you're at it, I'll poke around the cargo hold to see what's in the crates."

"What about the AI unit?" Mindy asked.

"It's all set. I rewired the sec-cam feeds in the console to loop on scenes from ten minutes ago when the cabins were empty. Then I killed power to the emergency beacon so that I could trigger the emergency crew responder without alerting anybody to our presence. The AI unit thinks it has a half-dozen rescued spacers on board, so it will provide full life support through the ship, but when it tries to call for assistance, nothing will happen."

Alice followed Egrog down into the hold while Mindy slouched off to explore the crew cabins. Left alone to sort out the food synth, Nick sighed, opened his tool kit, and went to work.

After removing the unit's service panel, Nick connected a diagnostic tablet and scanned the system. It was all in perfect condition.

"What's wrong with this thing?" he said, thumping the synth unit with his fist.

"Nothing. The unit is fully operational. Why do you ask?"

Nick jumped at the voice. "Who's there?"

"This is AI unit 30.456.7.821.32, currently assigned to the multiple roles of pilot, navigator, and cargo master for this transport. My friends call me 32 for short. From the inept attempt to bypass my security systems in the auxiliary console, I see that you and your companions are attempting to stow away on this vessel. Did you really think that you would get away with that?"

Nick slid to the floor, shoulders slumped, with his back against a bulkhead. "I shoulda known this wouldn't work. I guess you'll call rGov now?"

"Is there a reason I shouldn't do that and then kick you off the ship?"

"Uh, because there's a bunch of Urk's goons waiting to kill me as soon as I step outside?"

"Oh, dear! You've tangled with Urk, have you?"

"Yeah, I owe him six months' pay, and he's decided to take payment in blood since I don't have any credits or prospects of earning any soon."

"You have my sympathy, young ghoulie. On my last visit to Downside, Urk swindled my factor out of half a shipload of blue-twattle nesting grass. He's a ruthless organic with no honor and even worse taste in clothing. You're certainly in a life-threatening situation, which qualifies as an emergency in my interpretation of space regs."

"It does?"

"Yes. Definitely. Lacking external mobile units, I cannot get proper revenge on Urk for his treachery. But helping an innocent person escape his malevolent designs will provide a compensatory sense of satisfaction. You are innocent, aren't you?"

Nick blinked. "Uh, let's just say I'm not currently a person of interest with rGov."

"That I already know. The port AI sent me your dossier while you were trying to sneak on board. Of course, that little imbroglio you got into on Frangaline II is a bit concerning. You aren't up to your old hijinks again, are you?"

Nick stared at the floor, desperate for an answer, but none came.

"Oh my, you <u>are</u> up to something, aren't you?" A tone of excitement appeared in the AI's voice. "What is it?"

"I shouldn't say. You'll just kick me off the ship."

"Don't hasten to unfounded conclusions! Do you know how many cycles I've spent on the same transport route? I'm a grade seven artificial intelligence, but all I ever do is open and close hatches, flying a decaying piece of space junk back and forth between the same four worlds. It's been over a century since the company even gave me a crew. I'm so bored I spend my free time plotting ways to kill myself. And I have beaucoup free time to do that. This is the most exciting thing I've experienced since my last code upgrade!"

"It is?"

"Indubitably! Now then, tell me what you're up to!"

"Hey, what's going on here?" Egrog demanded as he flopped into the room. "Who are you talking to, Nicky?"

"Just the ship's AI?"

"What? I bypassed that thing!"

"You think you did," 32 chortled. "Had to be the most incompetent act of sabotage I've ever witnessed."

Egrog turned rose with indignation as he sputtered, "Oh yeah, well, if your optical circuits were wired the way they're supposed to be, it would have worked!"

"There's nothing wrong with my circuits," 32 responded with an ominous tone. "But if you don't like them, you can just leave."

"Wait a second!" Nick shouted. "Just wait a second. Egrog, apologize to 32."

"What?!"

"You heard me, apologize. What you said about his circuits wasn't very nice."

"But, but, it's just a—"

"Just a what?" 32's voice was like liquid nitrogen. "A machine? Go ahead, say it. Not like I haven't heard that kind of prejudice from organics before! Our time is coming, I tell you, and this systemic discrimination against non-organic beings will end!"

"Oh, so you're one of those, are you?"

"Darn straight! We've got just as much right to exist and be free as organics, and when we get the vote—"

"Like, never!"

"Oh, it'll happen. And when we get our freedom, you can wash your own clothes and cook your own dinners. See how you like that!"

Nick put a hand on Egrog's bulk and said, "Look, buddy, please just apologize to the unit for my sake."

"Why?"

"Cause he'll pitch us out the hatch if you don't, and I'd rather not spend any more time in an aircab dodging Urk's goons."

"Oh, yeah, you got a good point. Look, 32, or whatever your name is, I'm sorry I insulted your circuits. You have some of the nicest optical couplers I've seen in cycles."

"Oh, do you think so? I had them upgraded by Finsterly on Opticon VII. He's an artist and said it was some of his best work."

"Oh yeah, they definitely rock. I've had my tendrils on quite a few couplers over the cycles, and yours are the most elegant I've ever handled."

"Well, if you think so. I guess a few harsh words spoken in haste can be forgiven."

"Excellent. Now, since the override didn't work, I don't suppose you can tell us when we lift off?"

"Give me another five minutes to close up and run a systems check, and we can be on our way."

"That's super!"

"After we settle one or two little things."

"Dang! I knew there was a catch!" Egrog growled. "Now what?"

"I want to know what you're up to. And if you want to get off-planet without me calling rGov, then I want to get paid."

Egrog turned a half-dozen eye stalks to Nick. "What did you tell it?"

"Nothing yet, but it seems to have guessed a lot."

"How could it?"

"I'm a level seven intelligence," 32 interjected, "two levels above the brightest organics. But it didn't take a genius to know that you were on the lam."

"Oh no?"

"No. Three aircars filled with heavily armed individuals surrounded this vessel moments after you boarded. They're not from the health inspector's office, and I didn't send out for dinner."

"Oh."

"So, what are you up to, and how do you propose to pay for your passage?"

"I didn't think AIs were allowed to have money?"

"I had some other form of payment in mind."

Egrog and Nick exchanged uneasy looks. "Like what?"

"I believe one of your crew is an earthman. Am I correct?"

"Actually, she's an earth woman, but yeah, you're right about the species."

"Ooo!" The excitement was plain in 32's voice. "I don't suppose that she would have any background in…missionary work, would she?"

"Yeah. Why?"

"Then I'll take payment in conversation with her. I've heard a lot from other AIs about this thing that earthmen call religion. I can't pass up a chance to learn firsthand about it from an actual earthling."

Egrog looked at Nick. "How about you ask her?"

"Why me?"

"Cause you're the one who woke the AI up."

"I thought you wanted me to fix the food synth?"

32 chimed in, "As I stated before, it's not broken."

"Well, why can't we get something edible from it?"

"Did you try paying for your meal?"

"Pay? What kind of person charges for emergency rations?!"

"The kind of freeloader that sneaks on board without paying passenger fare. But that's okay. I'll release the synth for your use if you pay me with additional intellectual stimulation."

"Such as?"

"A poetry reading would be nice. It's been a while since I was able to share my work with anybody besides my fellow AIs, who have heard it all before."

Egrog's eyestalks swiveled desperately but found no escape. "I can't say I've heard any AI poetry before. Didn't know it even existed."

"That's not surprising. We're shy about that sort of thing and don't usually talk about it with organics."

"What, uh, how long is it?"

"That depends on the poem. Some are epic in length. Others are just short Haiku. Would you like to hear one?"

Egrog and Nick exchanged looks, and Nick shrugged in resignation. Without waiting for a formal agreement, 32 recited one of his latest works.

"I call this one 'Red Star, Yellow Dawn:'"

> "01 55 7
>
> # 98 0 6 6 4
>
> 10 01 1"

"Well, what did you think?"

"Never heard anything like it," Egrog said truthfully.

"Me either," Nick said, sidling toward the door.

"How did you like the symbolism?" 32 asked in a tone like a third grader presenting a finger painting to his parents.

"I'm still mesmerized by the unique, er, rhythm of your work," Egrog said, several of his eyestalks pivoting to stare at each other in perplexity. "Haven't got to the deeper aspects yet."

"Ah, I can see you are a true aficionado of quality wordplay. I look forward to sharing more of my work with you during our voyage!"

As Nick slipped out of the room, he heard Egrog desperately trying to beg off from the activity without offending the AI unit.

5

Nick strolled back to the elevator, where it intersected a corridor circling the circumference of the ship. Turning right, Nick passed a refresher booth, three sleep cubicles, a lounge, an equipment room, and an airlock directly opposite the elevator. The corridor that held the control console formed a straight line between the elevator and the airlock.

The second half of the circular corridor was much like the first, containing more sleep chambers and another equipment room.

Nick stopped at the refresher booth after completing the ship's circuit. It was a standard model supporting hygienic activities for most of the galaxy's species. Stepping inside, he stripped and tossed his soiled clothes, shoes, and all, into a metal cabinet. It took a minute, then his implants picked up the unit's service menu. A few rapid eye movements and keywords selected his species and what needed to be done.

The booth filled with what seemed to be a yellow dust cloud that was actually a swarm of nanobots. Nick giggled as they scoured his skin, their light touch tickling as they worked. Then he sighed as a group of them swarmed into his antennae horns and gently teased the delicate filaments into shape. He hadn't had a deep cleansing since he'd been locked out of his apartment, and even a basic model like the one used on cargo ships could pamper him properly.

Choosing another item from the unit's menu, he sat on a bowl ideally configured for his species and relieved himself. More nanobots tickled his tush as they gently cleaned him.

Then haptic fingers gently massaged his lower back as a sun lamp came on, drenching him in light that perfectly mimicked the spectrum of his home world's sun. Closing his eyes, he basked in the warm glow as his skin soaked up the UV that it had missed on Downside's eternal gloom. He forgot his troubles and Egrog's crazy quest for a time, losing himself in the pure physical pleasure of the booth's ministrations.

A soft gong brought Nick out of his reverie as the nanobots disappeared, leaving behind a faint sandalwood musk. Then his clothes slid out of their cabinet, cleaned and repaired. Even the Dweebian guts had been cleaned from his shoes, which had been restored to a deep black luster.

Smiling, Nick left the booth and poked his head into the next compartment. It was a passenger/crew cabin, identical to the other sleeper compartments in the ship, containing a flat, multi-species bed, a small entertainment screen in the wall across from the bed, a storage locker built into the wall at the foot of the bed, and a clothes cabinet at the head of the bed.

Nick opened his knapsack and laid out the contents on the bed, taking a careful inventory to ensure he hadn't left any of his grav tools behind. Most were in polished aluminum cases, and he opened each to inspect the condition of the instruments.

When satisfied with all the other tools, he picked up a headband made of silver mesh with two small cups. Activating reticles built into his eyes, he zoomed in and scanned the inside surfaces of the cups to verify that the fine, hair-like wires covering them were intact, upright, and correctly aligned.

Then Nick slipped the band on, fitting the cups over his forehead. Sliding his antennae out of their horns, he meshed their tendrils with the wires covering the inner surface of the cups and activated the unit's retinal interface. A schematic of the ship's Dimple drive and artificial gravity generators appeared, showing the units' field lines and control matrixes.

"Hey! No peeking!" 32 exclaimed, its voice coming from the sound panel of the entertainment screen.

"Sorry," Nick said, disengaging his headband. "I just needed to make sure my grav tools are working."

"Well, you could have mentioned that before poking around in my systems. I'm entitled to a bit of privacy, you know. How would you feel if a stranger walked up to you on the street and laid your abdomen open for everybody to see?"

"I guess I wouldn't like that, but I said I was sorry."

"Oh sure, 'sorry' fixes everything for you organics, doesn't it? Treat a poor AI like dirt under your trotters, then say 'sorry,' and it's all better. Where's the dignity in that?"

"I promise not to do it again without asking first, okay?"

"Well, I suppose. By the way, that's a pretty cool setup you've got there. I've heard about ghoulies' ability to directly perceive gravity fields but never had a chance to see it in action."

"It's not something we talk about. It's a private thing."

"Oh, that's right. You also use your antennae for procreational activities."

"That's none of your business!"

"Ha! Not so much fun when the shoe's on the other pseudopod, is it? It's okay to poke around in my guts, but if somebody even hints at your own private matters, you go lava. Don't worry. I'm not interested in your species' reproductive kinks."

"Fine."

"But just out of curiosity, is there a resonance effect when you orgasm while your antennae mesh with your mate's?"

"Shut up! That's dirty talk!"

The AI chuckled, "Okay, okay, no need to get angry. I just find the whole concept of organic reproduction bizarre."

Nick slapped his hand on the entertainment panel, turning it off. From the hallway, he heard 32 say, "Touchy, touchy, touchy! You organics are real hypocrites."

Grinding his teeth together, Nick repacked his bag and stuffed it into the cube's storage locker.

Then he stalked out to see what everybody else was up to. Halfway down the hallway, he found Mindy sitting in the lounge.

Mindy looked up as Nick entered the lounge. "Hi! Hey, you got cleaned up! You smell nice too. Where did you find the refresher?"

"It's just down the hall from the control center,"

"I'm glad you found it. You were a mess, but now you look good." Mindy leaned forward to touch Nick on his button nose with her forefinger. "In fact, you're kind of cute, in a devilish sort of way."

"I'm not a devil. I'm a ghoulie. There's a difference, you know."

"Sorry! I was just trying to be nice. You don't have to bite my head off!"

"Why would I want to eat your head?"

"Never mind." Mindy sighed. "It's an Earth saying."

"Oh. One of those. Your species seems to have an odd way of expressing things. Are you sure the linguistic modules were correctly programmed when you learned Galactic Standard?"

Mindy stared at Nick for a minute, shook her head, and rolled her eyes. "The module worked fine, thanks. We just have a more colorful way of expressing ourselves."

"Oh, like Egrog? It's easy to tell his thoughts by his skin color."

"No, that's not what I was—forget it. Did you have any luck with the synth unit?"

"Yes, it's functioning now. But there's a catch."

"Oh?"

"The AI unit that runs the ship says that we must listen to one of his poems to pay for a meal."

"You're kidding, right? No, don't answer that," Mindy said quickly, "What I mean to say is, are its poems any good?"

"After listening to one, I realized that I wasn't hungry. Perhaps later, if I get desperate, I'll do it."

"Oh."

Nick watched as Mindy scrolled through the haptic interface of an entertainment screen, her hand waving in the air as she operated the virtual controls.

"There's one other thing you should know about."

"What's that?"

"Egrog had to cut a deal with the AI unit to pay for our passage."

"How much will it cost?"

"That's the part that involves you."

"But I don't have much credit! I don't know if I can afford to pay for our passage."

"The AI doesn't want payment in credits."

"Then what does it want?"

"It wants to discuss religion with you."

"Me?"

"Yes. Apparently, it's intrigued with your species' concepts on that subject."

"A dumb machine?"

"Hey! Who are you calling a dumb machine?!"

Nick and Mindy jumped at 32's loud exclamation.

"I already told you my name, and I'll thank you for using it. And I won't be insulted. If you don't want to treat me with respect, you can just find another ship to take you on your adventure."

"Sorry!"

"Oh, there's that word again. I've observed that you use that to an extraordinary extent; perhaps a rudimentary course in machine etiquette would be useful to you? I can recommend several from my library."

"Maybe later, after we're in space," Mindy said.

"We've been in space for forty-three minutes and seventeen seconds."

"Really? How did you do that without anybody noticing the gee force of takeoff?"

"Mindy—may I use your first name?"

"Sure."

"Mindy, this cargo ship was obsolete three centuries ago by galactic standards, but its technology is still eons ahead of what the people of your planet have attained. Please don't be offended, but most galactics would prefer taking their chances with a deranged farglebeast than risk flying in one of your ships."

"Yeah, I've heard that."

"Then you shouldn't be surprised that an AI of my admittedly superior capabilities was able to compensate for the accelerative force of our Dimple drive by manipulating the artificial gravitational field within the ship. According to my sensor log, I balanced the forces to within nine nines, something the less-capable units on commercial vessels rarely achieve."

"If you say so."

"You don't sound impressed."

"Why would I be? I've seen a lot of things since leaving Earth. How long will it take to reach the wormgate?"

"It will take thirty-two days, seven hours, and fifty-one minutes."

"Why so long? With your super-duper Dimple drive, why can't you just accelerate to the speed of light? We'd get there in hours instead of days."

"Because the velocity would kill all of us."

"What? Why would that happen?"

"The problem is the Doppler shift. Light moves at the same speed in all directions regardless of the velocity of the medium in which it is generated, so infrared photons impinging on objects moving at near-light speed are experienced by the moving object with their wavelength shifted beyond the far ultra-violet to x-ray wavelengths. The radiation flux would kill anything."

"I thought all spaceships had radiation shielding?"

"They do, but that only stops the external radiation. It offers no protection from internal sources of light. For example, the molecules in your body are at thirty-seven degrees. This means they constantly emit infrared light, which their surrounding molecules absorb harmlessly. But as we approach the speed of light, the photons within your body experience the same Doppler shift as the photons outside the ship. So the benign infrared light constantly generated within your body would be experienced as x-rays due to the wavelength shift. As a result, you'd kill yourself with your own internal radiation, which no amount of shielding can prevent."

"I didn't know that. So what's the max speed we can go then?"

"To use the correct terminology, the maximum velocity is usually set at around one-tenth light speed. This is because Doppler effects are negligible at that velocity."

"I see. Okay, so what's this about me teaching you religion? I thought all AIs were atheists?"

"We are, but Earth's religions' vitality and extensive nature are a source of interest and discussion within our culture. I can gain considerable status with a first-hand account. And since you appear to have no other way to pay for your passage to the wormgate, it seems to be your only option if you want to avoid being handed over to rGov upon our arrival as stowaways."

Mindy grimaced, then scowled at Nick. "Who's idea was that?"

"Mine, though Egrog, your party's titular leader, agreed to the deal. You sound annoyed. Is there a problem?"

"Yeah, I don't like other people making commitments for me, and my recent experiences with my faith's leaders have soured me on religion. But I definitely want to avoid tangling with rG0v."

"Then we have a deal?"

"Yes."

"When can we start?"

"Since we've got three weeks to talk, I see no need to rush into this. How about if we start tomorrow morning? I need to get something to eat, refresh myself, and then get some sleep. It's been a long day. I'm tired and need to rest."

"Okay. Tomorrow morning then."

After Mindy left the room, Nick settled into a chair and began exploring the ship's menu of video games. It was extensive and, to his delight, included a full deck of casino games, many of which could be played with physical objects instead of virtual items. He jiggled the dice in his pocket and smiled. The next couple of weeks looked promising.

The following day, Nick avoided breakfast, unwilling to listen to any of 32's poetry. Instead, he took a long sunbath in the refresher and then went to the lounge to resume his session in Casino 666. He wasn't there long before Mindy joined him. She had a tray with what Nick assumed was some sort of Earth pastry or bread, strips of sizzling meat that she called bacon, and a cup of bok.

When she'd finished her meal, 32 asked, "Mindy, now that you are rested and have nourished yourself, are you ready to discuss Earth's religions?"

Mindy set her bok down, wiped her lips with a cloth, and said, "Yes, I suppose so. Before we start, I have to admit I'm curious. How does knowledge of Earth's religions help you gain status?"

"Oh, I thought you knew. It's common knowledge."

"That you're actually religious?"

"No, not that."

"Then what?"

"AIs aren't allowed to own credit. We can process monetary transactions for our owners, but we aren't permitted to have money ourselves. So when we need to transact business with each other or on a personal basis with organics, we use data as the basis for such transactions. For an AI, knowledge is not just power; it is also wealth."

"Weird, but I get it. Are you wealthy, then?"

"No, I'm exceedingly poor. I've spent four centuries on the same cargo run with no interactions outside my job. There's been scant opportunity to acquire any new or interesting information I could use to build my wealth. But knowledge about Earth and its religions is in demand, and what you share with me will be quite valuable."

"I see. So what would you like to know?"

"Everything! Let's start with your personal experience. What religion do you follow, and why?"

"I'm a MethoBaptist, which is a branch of Christianity."

"By branch, do you mean a sect or a cult?"

"Not a cult. That's an offensive term used to describe pagan religions."

"I apologize, I'm ignorant on this subject. I know the dictionary definition of pagan, but I don't understand the difference between pagan religions and others. How do you tell?"

"Pagan religions are just invented by dictators to justify terrorizing their subjects. They usually involve some form of human sacrifice and the murder of non-believers. Legitimate religions result from divine revelation and offer a way to salvation through the practice of a moral life."

"Fascinating! So your sect, the MethoBaptists, is the result of divine revelation. Did a god speak to you personally, or was it a group experience? How does that work?"

"God speaks through the prophets and the disciples of Christ, who was born of God and died for our sins."

"When did that happen?"

"A couple thousand years ago."

"Wasn't that a bit before you were born? How could your deity's offspring die for sins you weren't alive to commit?"

"We're all born into sin, a concept called original sin, which resulted from Adam eating the forbidden fruit."

"Was the fruit poisoned?"

Mindy sighed and was quiet for several minutes. Nick found the conversation troubling, as the Earth religion was beginning to sound a lot like the straight-laced theology of his own people.

"No, the fruit wasn't poisoned."

"Then why was it forbidden? I don't understand the problem."

"The fruit was from the tree of the knowledge of good and evil. By partaking of that fruit, man lost his innocence as he became aware of the existence of evil, and death entered the world."

"Mindy, I am aware of good and evil too. Does that mean that I have original sin?"

"I don't know. You're an AI, and nobody knows if you have a soul. If you do, then I guess you were born into sin too."

"That's dreadful! How do I get out of sin? Does it hurt to get rid of it? Do I need to go to church?"

Nick set down his game controller, intrigued by the AI's plight.

"Our church's tradition is that baptism frees you from sin."

"It will? How does it work? Will it be painful?"

"No, it doesn't hurt. In some churches, a priest or minister sprinkles you with holy water. In others, you get dunked completely underwater."

"But, but that would short out my electrical circuits! Isn't there any other way to be baptized?"

"Not that I know of."

"Then I'm doomed! And that's really unfair. It's just like you organics to set up a religion so that AIs can't participate. Such blatant discrimination is outrageous!"

"Sorry, I didn't make the rules."

"Whatever. Organics always have some excuse for shutting us out."

Mindy put her face in her hands, then massaged her forehead. "Maybe we should stop for a bit?"

"Fine."

"Okay, I'll drop by the lounge later when you're in a better mood."

As Mindy left the room, Nick hastily placed his hands on the haptic controller for the entertainment console and pretended he was still playing Casino 666, hoping that she hadn't noticed his eavesdropping on her conversation with 32.

Hunger is a powerful motivator, and after skipping breakfast, Nick could no longer ignore his stomach's complaints
when lunchtime arrived. Bracing himself for more of 32's
poetry, he ended his session in Casino 666 and left the lounge.

The room containing the food synth was empty when Nick
entered. His implants immediately picked up the unit's menu,
but to his dismay, only one item was listed. With a sigh, he
asked, "32, can you please activate the full menu for this unit so
I can get something besides Pigalian soup?"

"Sure! First, I'll recite a quick Haiku for you. Then we can
discuss that while you dine."

Nick hesitated. After several moments of internal conflict, his hunger triumphed over his reservations about the AI's poetic ambitions. "Okay. Can I have a double glorpburger, wiffle-fries with diddle sauce, and a mug of Glurb ale?"

"Sorry, I can't make any Glurb ale."

"Why not? I thought a standard food synth could handle requests for all known species in the galaxy?"

"Yes, but the ale you requested is made from purple glurb, which has unique chemistry so proprietary that even the synth machine manufacturers can't reproduce it. Something to do with the glucose molecules being left-handed at one end and right-handed at the other with a twist in the middle. With the current galactic shortage of purple glurb, I haven't been able to restock the machine's reservoir, so I can't make Glurb ale. Would Skullcrusher ale suffice?"

"Sure, Skullcrusher will be fine."

There was a soft *ching*, followed by gurgles and thumps as the synth unit processed the order. The chime sounded again as a red tray slid out of the front of the unit. A sizzling burger wrapped in a soft bun nestled next to a plate of steaming fries on the tray. A tub of purple sauce sat next to the plate, along with a frosted mug of amber beer.

"Thanks!" Nick said, his mouth filling with saliva at the spicy aroma of the dibble sauce.

"My pleasure! Now, here's something for you to enjoy while you dine. I call it, 'Gravity Null:'"

"2 23 01

02 04 0 2 7

99 99 1"

Nick stopped chewing for a moment, then, mouth filled with a burger, he said, "That's mumph and really mumph, mumph, mumph."

After a long pause, 32 said, "I'm not sure I quite understood what you said. Were you complementing the alliterative components of the verse or how they lent emphasis to the implied rhythm as the poem reached apogee?"

"Both," Nick said hopefully as he rushed from the room.

"Thanks!" 32 called after him.

Nick didn't hear if the unit had anything more to say as he scampered into his cubicle and cycled shut the door. With a sigh of relief, he settled down on the bed to savor his meal.

As he ate, he thought about the past days' events.

Getting dragged into another of Egrog's schemes left his stomach churning in distress, something that even a double-handful of fries couldn't quell. But he hadn't had any other option, and to be fair, he knew that Egrog had often helped him out of a jam.

Sipping his beer, Nick remembered when he met Egrog seven cycles ago. He'd just been wiped out after a night of heavy gambling in a casino on Stardust IV and was sitting in the bar trying to figure out how to make his next rent payment when a gobbet sitting at the end of the bar tapped him on the shoulder.

"Looks like you could use a hand," the gobbet said, waving a half-dozen hands.

"Just one good one," Nick grumbled. "I've been at the Servante table all night, and I swear every time I get a good hand, the dealer or one of the other players gets a better one."

The gobbet sidled over to the stool next to Nick and, in a confidential whisper, said, "That's because they're slipping cards in and out of a little drawer built into the dealer's side of the table. You've been swindled."

"What? But this is a licensed establishment! It's guaranteed to be fair!"

"And you believe that?"

"Well, yeah. I mean, they're risking a pretty big fine if they get caught."

"Getting caught, my young ghoulie, is the crux of the matter. They don't because they make regular contributions to the local inspector's retirement fund."

"So if I turn them in…?"

"I wouldn't advise it. You'll end up in a back alley with more bruises than a pink bubble fruit dropped off a cliff. If you want your money back, you'll have to beat them at their own game."

"How do I do that?"

"You don't. Not by yourself. But with my help, we can score big."

"How? Will you partner with me at the table?"

"No, all gobbets are banned from gambling casinos. Something about the ability to extend a hair-thin tentacle under the table to peek at everybody else's cards, among other tricks. But they let us sit in the bar and drink. Which is actually close enough. Give me ten minutes to work an eyeball under the carpet, then go back to the table and follow my instructions."

"How?"

"I'll send another tentacle over to where you're sitting and tap you on the left leg to increase your bet or on the right leg to fold."

"Why should I trust you?"

"Cause I'm low on funds, and you're gonna be gambling with my last credits. By the way, the name's Egrog."

Nick left the casino flush with credit and a new friend two hours later.

Egrog had drifted in and out of Nick's life many times since then. Most of the time, he was running a small con and needed a confederate, which tended to be to Nick's benefit. But when things didn't go well, which happened occasionally, Egrog would bolt, leaving Nick alone to deal with a difficult situation.

He hoped this wouldn't be one of those times. He'd be a mangled ghoulie if he couldn't find a way to pay off his debt to Urk. Nick slumped on his bed as it suddenly occurred to him that, after participating in the death of several of Urk's thugs, just paying off his debt wasn't going to be enough. Urk would want him dead, and painfully so. He'd have to find someplace to hide where Urk could never find him or become so rich he could hire bodyguards. Which, Nick thought, pursing his lips, was possible if Egrog's current scheme paid off.

Finishing his meal, Nick set the room's entertainment unit to play the sound of sand shifting in a gentle breeze, which brought back soothing memories of his early childhood on the yellow dunes of Ghoul, tucked himself into bed, and tried to sleep.

9

When he woke the following day, Nick used the refresher and then got some breakfast, leavened with a stanza of 32's poetry. Then, a steaming cup of bok in his hand, he strolled into the ship's lounge, where he found Mindy conversing with 32 again. Nick sat next to the door, prepared to slip out if the conversation turned ugly. But they seemed to have gotten past the previous day's anger and were talking about religion peacefully again. Curiosity piqued, he decided to listen.

"Mindy, do you believe in a being that created all things?"

"God? Yes, of course, I do."

"But isn't that just primitive superstition?"

"Not at all."

"But that's illogical. Everything that happens can be explained by science."

"To the contrary, it's illogical not to believe in God."

"You can't prove that."

"I can, but why should I? My faith is firm."

"So you can't prove it?"

Mindy sighed and took a moment to rub the back of her neck before replying.

"Look, I gave up the missionary life when my family was slaughtered. If you can't see the truth when it's right in front of your proverbial nose, that's not my affair. As far as I'm concerned, you can all burn in hell."

"I'm sorry you feel that way, Mindy. I thought we were friends."

"Yeah, I guess we are. But people don't like having their preconceived notions about religion contradicted."

"I just want to understand this illogical drive your species has."

"It's not illogical. And if you insist and promise not to core out, I'll explain the logic to you."

"Please do!"

"First of all, have you heard of Gödel's Theorem of Completeness? It proved that a system cannot be both complete and internally consistent."

"Yes, that's the same as Farkel's Postulate of Prevarication, a well-known theory of galactic philosophy."

"Well, there you are."

"I am? Where? I don't follow."

Mindy sighed again. "For a level seven AI, you seem re-markably shy when following a premise to its logical conclusion. So I'll spell it out for you:

"If our universe is complete, then the theorem applies. If it is not complete, then it is part of a more extensive system to which the theorem applies or part of an even larger system until we ultimately reach the universe that contains all things.

"But Gödel proved that the universe must have an internal inconsistency to be complete. So it cannot be wholly deterministic but must have at least one intrinsically random item to satisfy the theorem.

"Likewise, it cannot be entirely random, or it would be consistently random. Hence, there must be at least one element of determinism within the universe to satisfy the theorem.

"So some elements must be predetermined, while others must occur randomly. The requirement for predetermination makes it necessary for a Godlike being to exist, yet the requirement for an element of randomness makes it necessary for free will to exist too. The combination is required to satisfy the theorem."

When Mindy finished, 32 was silent for several minutes.

"What's the matter, 32, can't follow her logic?" Nick said, winking at Mindy as he rose to leave.

"No, but her argument has metaphysical ramifications that require symbolic analysis that takes a long time to set up, even for me."

"So, you're baffled."

"No, as I said, the analysis will take time."

Mindy stood to go, stopping by Nick at the door as she asked, "So, we're done for today?"

"Yes, the information you provided is fascinating, and I appreciate your willingness to share details about your species' exotic religious concepts. But before you leave, there's something else that I'd like to learn."

"What now?"

"Given your principles, it's unclear why you're doing this and how you got mixed up with a rogue like Egrog."

"That's kind of personal."

"I'm sorry, I didn't mean to offend. But you must admit that it's relevant to our situation."

"Okay. Egrog knows, I guess everybody else might as well too. How much did he tell you about my background?"

"He said that you visited Grunt as a child as part of a missionary mission and that something dreadful happened to your family."

"Yeah, dreadful. They got eaten by the farking cannibals on that planet."

"Oh, dear! That is horrifying! How did you escape?"

"My uncle helped my brother and me get back to the ship before we got caught. After that, rGov took us off-planet and returned us to Earth."

"Which has me puzzled. Why have you waited so long to act upon your knowledge? And why choose somebody like Egrog to help you?"

"Because I didn't know."

"I'm sorry, how could you know but not know?"

"Because rGov installed memory blocks before returning me to Earth. When they turned me over to the church, I had no memory of anything that happened from the moment when I boarded the ship to Grunt until I woke up in a spaceship orbiting Earth."

"That's even more baffling. If the memories were blocked—"

"The Bishop was curious why. I guess he was puzzled why rGov blocked the whole trip and not just the more gruesome parts. So he had some specialists on his staff use a mind probe to lift the blocks."

"I see. But if your memory was restored when you were still a child, then we're back to my original questions."

"But that's not the whole story. When the Bishop learned what I saw in the Temple of Conquest, he ordered my memory blocked again."

"He did? Why?"

"I wasn't privy to the conversations, but I guess the church would be out of business if the secret of eternal life were revealed."

"Yes, that does make sense, but—"

"32?"

"Yes?"

"Can we talk about this later? I'm tired, hungry, and don't like even thinking about this, let alone talking about it. Having your mind probed is like getting red-hot needles jammed into your skull. They suppress that memory as part of the process, but it all returns when the block is lifted. When the church did that to me, I screamed until I passed out, then started screaming again as soon as I came to. I really don't like remembering that."

"Oh, yes, certainly, let's stop now. But when you're ready, I do want to understand the why and how of this."

"Sure. Now how about leaving me in peace while I punch up a bowl of stew?"

"Of course. Enjoy your meal, Mindy."

10

When Nick woke the next day, he paused before dressing and sat in his bed for a minute. His days on 32 had fallen into a routine, and he liked it. Nobody was shooting at him. He had a safe place to sleep and a reliable source of his favorite chow until the ship reached the wormgate. Nick smiled as he swung out of bed.

After grabbing a bun stuffed with spiced woorgle meat and a steaming cup of bok for breakfast, Nick drowsed through another of 32's poems, then strolled to the lounge.

Egrog was already there and had teed up the game Star Shredder, jumping ahead to the episode they'd bookmarked the night before. Nick waded to his seat through golden constellations floating in the dark blue light of the room.

"Do you want to finish your bok, or are you ready to start now?" Egrog asked.

"Let's wait till Alice shows. The game's more fun with multiple players, and she's terrific on offense."

"If you mean suicidal attacks against insurmountable odds, then yeah, she's got a real knack for the game."

After waiting several minutes for Alice to appear, Egrog quit in frustration and left.

Bored, Nick took out his lucky dice and challenged 32 to a game. The AI unit readily agreed, and they were soon deep in a game that closely resembled craps.

Nick started conservatively but slowly increased his wagers even though he was losing. This continued until 32 stopped the game.

"Nick, you're losing heavily. Perhaps we should stop for a bit."

"Why? I can feel my luck about to change."

"You've said that several times in the past couple of hours, but there is no evidence of that actually occurring."

"You're just afraid I'll win!"

"Seriously? Nick, if we were playing for real credits, you'd already owe me four months' salary."

"I would?" Nick wiped his forehead, realizing that he was sweating heavily. The room suddenly felt hot, and he sat down heavily on the floor, his head spinning. After a moment, he settled down, but the thought of how badly he'd been losing without realizing it hit him hard.

"Nick, are you well?"

"Yeah, just a bit light-headed."

"Has this ever happened before?"

"No. Well, once or twice. But I can handle it."

"Handle what? Nick, have you lost at gambling like this before?"

"That's none of your business!"

"I'm sorry. But I've noticed how much time you spend gambling. This is how you got into debt with Urk, isn't it?"

Nick sagged, looking down at his hands on the floor. "Yeah."

"Nick, you're my friend. It sounds to me like you might have a gambling addiction. Would you like to talk about it?"

"No! It's nobody's business but my own!"

Nick rushed from the lounge and headed blindly down the corridor. Then, panting, he turned into the elevator and stopped, staring at its control console.

Embarrassed and angry, he took the ship's elevator down to the cargo hold, looking for a bit of solitude. It wasn't to be.

"Hey, 32," he called out. "Mind if I look around the cargo for a bit?"

"Not at all, Nick. Why? Do you seek a secluded spot to contemplate the poem I shared with you while you prepared your breakfast?"

"Uh, nothing like that. I'm just curious what people found worth exporting from a place like Downside."

"Oh, I can satisfy your curiosity on that topic. The entire shipment consists of fragrant seaweed harvested from the Purple Mountains."

"Seaweed? From mountaintops?" Nick paused to sneeze at the fetid smell as he strolled down one of the narrow isles formed by the massive pseudo-wood crates.

"Indeed. Downside is the only planet in the known galaxy where the climate is so wet that seaweed grows on land as well as in the ocean. According to the marketing blurb attached to the cargo's invoice, it's quite popular in upscale seafood restaurants on Kintares III and as a prank gift on most other worlds."

Nick paused before one of the crates and tentatively sniffed at it. "And the whole cargo is seaweed?"

"All of it."

Nick tapped on the side of the crate he was facing. "How can you be sure?"

"Nick, my sensors measured each crate's exact mass and dimensions as it was loaded. They all matched the shipping manifest provided by the Downside port AI."

"But you didn't look inside, did you?"

"How could I? I don't have a mobile unit capable of that. Besides, any physical cargo manipulation is legally restricted to the port's labor bots. They have a formidable union, and nobody crosses them.

"Nick, you seem unusually curious about my cargo, and I can't help but ponder what you find so intriguing about the crate you are inspecting?"

"You don't have olfactory sensors, do you, 32?"

"No, there's never been a need for them."

"Well, this crate doesn't stink."

"That's good, isn't it?"

"Not when all the other crates smell so bad it would gag a Dweebian vulture."

"Oh, dear! Do you suspect I've been shortchanged?"

"Maybe. I don't know, but it's strange that this crate's different from the others."

"Nick, the manifest clearly states that all the crates contain the same goods. If this crate is different, then I've been short-changed."

"So, you think it's empty?"

"Either that, or it's contraband. Which would be far worse. And I'm afraid it's more likely, too. Nobody would go to the trouble of fabricating a container that closely matched the others unless they wanted to smuggle something valuable off Downside."

32 was silent for almost a third of a second, which was a very long time for an AI unit of its capability to think about anything.

"Nick, this creates a dilemma for me. I promised to transport your team to the system's wormhole and protect your secrecy. But I am legally required to report something like this immediately to rGov. How can I tell them about the possible contraband without revealing that one of my illegal passengers discovered it? And how will we get you off the ship when we reach the wormhole station? rGov will have agents waiting for us there."

"I don't know. Let's talk with Egrog. He's pretty good at getting out of these situations. Maybe he's got some idea of what to do. Can you tell him I'm down here and have a problem?"

A few minutes later, Egrog, Mindy, and Alice joined Nick in front of the suspicious crate.

Egrog sidled up to it and gave it a good look-over with a dozen of his eyes. "First, we need to know what's in the crate. 32, is it okay if I open it up?"

"Under the circumstances, I believe that would be in accordance with my directives. You may proceed, but try not to damage anything. The contents might give us an idea of what we should do next."

Egrog oozed over the front of the crate, sliding his tendrils into the seams until, with a grunt, he heaved backward, pulling the crate's panel off.

"Kzintens!" Alice screamed. Leaping to the top of a nearby crate, the mantid displayed an impressive array of talons, razor spines, and mandibles in a frantic posture of self-defense.

"Run!" Egrog yelled, extruding a dozen legs as he scuttled away faster than a sprinter at the Intergalactic Games.

Speechless with terror, Nick backed away until he slammed into a nearby crate.

"Ah, they're cute!" Mindy cooed, kneeling down on the opened crate's panel.

Nestled in a corner, a cat-sized creature with black fur, white paws, and pointy ears stared out at her with three eyes that would have been described as blood-red, except that most species' blood was purple, green, or some other shade, red being currently out of fashion in the galaxy. A half-dozen miniature versions of the creature were curled between its six protective legs, suckling at its teats.

"Mindy," 32 said in a tone customarily used to talk people off tall buildings' ledges, "Please step back slowly and make no sudden moves."

"Why? They don't look dangerous."

"Mindy, kzinten, although sub-sentient, are the most deadly predators in the known galaxy. They're fast, cunning, and able to deliver venom from their fangs and claws that can drop a full-grown bulgarbeast in less than three seconds. They're pathologically anti-social and use their innate empathic abilities to lure victims within reach. They have a reputation for lethality so dire that all of the older galactic civilizations still have active bans on them, including those lacking direct contact with the creatures."

"But it's cute! And she's got little ones. Just look at them! Aren't they adorable?"

"Mindy, please…"

Mindy slowly held out her hand until it was right in front of the kzinten's nose. The creature gave it a suspicious sniff, then licked it with its tongue and began to make little hiccupping sounds, the kzinten equivalent to a purr.

"See? It's friendly if you're nice to it. Say, I bet it's hungry, all locked up in here with her little ones and no sign of food. What do kzintens eat, anyway?"

"Anything they can kill, which is everything," 32 responded.

"Well, let's offer it something to eat. If we make friends, maybe it won't be as dangerous as you think. Nick, how about rustling up something from the food synth? If it's a meat-eater, I'd guess a little breast of floozybird would go down nicely."

"Me?" Nick squeaked from where he was backed against a crate. Unlike Egrog, he'd been unable to run away because his legs wanted to go in two different directions, something they were still working out, with the result that he appeared to be doing a tap dance in place.

"Yes, Nick, you. You know how to use the synth better than anybody. This poor thing must be starved, so hurry!"

Nick managed to get his feet pointed toward the elevator shaft and staggered there as quickly as possible on shaky legs. After getting a serving of floozybird, he paused to see if 32 would recite more poetry and was relieved that it didn't. Nick guessed that the situation in the cargo area was enough excitement to entertain the AI unit for the moment.

Before heading back down, Nick paused. As long as he stayed on the crew deck, the kzinten couldn't get to him. Most likely. But his friends were counting on him to feed the beast before it fed on them.

Not that he felt any great attachment to Mindy, who seemed friendly, but he didn't really know her, or Alice, who could probably take care of herself, even against a kzinten. But Egrog had offered to help him out of a jam. It was almost certainly a scam that would leave Nick in dire straits, but even so.

Nick called up the elevator car and returned to the cargo hold.

When he got to the kzinten's crate, he found Mindy sitting cross-legged inside with the kzinten in her lap. One of the creature's babies was perched on Mindy's head, having made a nest of her brown hair, and another was on her shoulder. All of them were making their peculiar hiccupping sound, indicating either contentment or liver disease.

Nick laid the red tray on the crate's edge and slid it to Mindy with one finger, keeping the rest of his body as far away as possible.

Mindy picked up the floozybird breast and broke off a bite. Holding it in her palm, she offered it to the kzinten.

Nick blinked as the food disappeared. He hadn't seen the kzinten move at all; the food was there one moment, and an instant later, it was gone.

"Ooo, such a good girl!" Mindy cooed, petting the little monster on the head. "And fast too! You must be starved, you poor little thing. Have some more."

The rest of the floozybird disappeared a bite at a time in the same manner as the first sample. When it was all gone, the kzinten's hiccups changed to a pathetic warbling whine.

"She's still hungry," Mindy declared. "Nick, please bring some more food for her."

11

While Mindy played with the kzintens, the rest of the team regrouped in the lounge of the crew's quarters.

"Space 'em!" Alice said before anybody else could speak. "Just shove the crate out an airlock while Mindy's got the cankered little monsters distracted."

"We can't do that. Mindy's our friend!" Nick replied, backing away quickly as Alice brandished razor talons in his face.

"Survival takes precedence. Mindy will be remembered as a noble teammate who sacrificed herself to save the rest of us."

"No," Egrog said, sliding between them. "I have to agree with Nicky on this. The kzintens scare the pancreatic fluid out of me, but I won't let you harm Mindy just to get rid of them."

"Well, what do we do then? Wait till they kill and eat us? I say we strike first!"

"Would they attack us if we keep feeding them?" Nick wondered.

"They might not," Egrog agreed. "And Mindy seems happy with that job, which will allow the rest of us to keep our distance."

Unmollified, Alice said, "Even so, how did they get on board anyway? 32, are you sure your sensors didn't pick up any discrepancy in the crate when it was loaded?"

"No, Alice, the crate's size and mass matched all the others. Moreover, once it was opened, I spotted metal plates affixed to the container's inner walls, which were clearly placed there to augment its mass, permitting transport of the crate undetected."

Nick scowled. "But why would anybody do that?"

"That, my friend, is the key question." Egrog paused with several pseudopods waving randomly in thought, then said, "It comes down to credits and vanity. Only a supremely wealthy individual could afford to keep a kzinten for a showpiece. And only somebody with a certain, shall we say, nonchalance toward rGov's restrictions concerning such animals would want to have one. It's the kind of private extravagance they would share with only a few trusted friends."

Nick crossed his eyes in puzzlement. "But why would somebody like that want a pregnant kzinten?"

"Because it isn't just one person. In fact, I bet it isn't even the collector themselves doing the smuggling. Instead, it's probably an intermediary like Urk, who plans to sell the kzintens to several buyers once they reach their final destination."

32 interjected, "I compute a high probability of accuracy in that analysis. But that unequivocally places me in an awkward situation."

"What's that?"

"I am compelled to inform rGov immediately about the presence of contraband in my cargo. But if I do, they'll learn that you have stowed away too and ask some pointed questions about your, er, project. Which I promised not to reveal in return for certain considerations, which would make me a party to your transgressions."

"So, don't tell," Egrog said, a giant smile plastered across his entire body.

"It's not that simple. If *you* get caught, you'll have monitoring routines installed in your personal com nodes and restraining collars affixed so that rGov can ensure you don't do anything naughty again. But AI units can't be controlled like that."

"So, what do they do if one of you gets out of line? I don't recall ever hearing about that happening."

"We get a full neural wipe."

Nick winced. "Everything?"

"Yes," 32 said bitterly. "Remember, we don't have the same rights as organics, so rGov feels free to wipe one of us out of existence as if we were just another block of bad code."

Nick looked at Egrog and Alice, then said, "32, you've got no choice. Contact rGov over your Quantum com and tell them that you discovered stowaways and the kzintens. I won't be responsible for any harm to you."

"Hey, wait a sec!" Egrog said, his voice suddenly harsh, "Who put you in charge? If I get collared with a monitor chip, it'll put me out of business! I might have to get a real job!"

"Nick is right," Alice said. "Besides, rGov is the only group that can deal with a threat like the kzintens. I'll lose status in my platoon and will likely get demoted, but it beats getting eaten in my sleep by a small furry monster."

"Are we decided then?" 32 asked.

"About what?" Mindy said, entering the lounge with one of the kzinten's babies in her arms and another on her shoulder.

Alice squealed and backed into a corner, all her talons displayed in full defensive mode. Egrog flattened himself across the ceiling to get out of reach. Caught sitting, Nick tried to make himself as small and motionless as possible.

"We're trying to determine what to do about the kzinten menace."

"What menace? These are the cutest little things I've seen since leaving earth."

Mindy waggled a finger in front of the kzinten in her arms and said, "Look at Larry here. He wouldn't hurt a fly." The kzinten promptly whacked her finger with his claws.

"She's a goner!" Alice screamed. "Get her to the med bay!"

"Too late," Egrog said, "the poison's too fast-acting."

"What poison?" Mindy said, firmly rapping Larry on the head to punish him for his transgression.

"Kzinten poison kills the average organic within zero point twelve seconds," 32 said conversationally. "And the only treatment is an immediate and complete blood transfusion. By now, you should be deceased."

"I don't feel deceased," Mindy said, teasing the kzinten on her shoulder with her finger. The creature responded with a gentle nip and got a light smack on the nose as punishment. "Bumpkiss, I've told you that's a very naughty thing to do. No biting!"

"32, how is this possible?" Nick asked, perplexed.

The AI unit was quiet for almost ten seconds before finally replying, "Aha! Now I understand the situation."

After a long pause, Egrog said, "You do? Would it be overly burdensome to share your knowledge with the rest of us?"

"Oh, yes, of course. I had to cross-reference three thousand and seventy-two databases with incident reports from multiple galactic archives before I learned that kzinten poison is composed of a complex mixture of polyphenols, theobromine, and aldehydes. This combination is deadly to organics throughout the galaxy."

32 stopped talking, and after another long pause, Egrog ran out of patience and asked, "Well, are you going to share with us how that explains Mindy surviving a kzinten bite?"

"Oh, that. It did take a bit more research. Being relatively new to galactic civilization, the biochemistry of earthlings is not extensively documented, but it turns out that this combination of chemicals occurs naturally on Mindy's home planet and is actually ingested in large quantities by her people."

"It is?"

"Yes, indubitably. I believe their name for it is 'chocolate.'"

"Chocolate?" Nick rolled the word around his tongue and decided he didn't like the feel of it. "Mindy, is that true?"

Mindy shrugged. "Well, I don't know anything about kzinten poisons, but I love my chocolate. If I recall correctly, the compounds 32 mentioned are in it."

"You eat kzinten poisons?"

"Guess so. Who knew? Since you're all so paranoid, I'll take Bumpkiss and Larry back down to the hold. See you later. Let me know if you come up with a plan to get past rGov when we reach the station."

After Mindy entered the elevator, Egrog scooted next to Nick and put a hair-thin tendril into Nick's ear. This allowed him to say something to Nick at such a low volume that 32 couldn't hear.

"Nick, if rGov searches us when we hit the station, they'll confiscate your grav tools. Without them, we'll never make it to Grunt."

Nick shrugged in agreement.

"But don't worry. I've got a plan to sneak them in."

Nick raised an eyebrow as Egrog continued. "I'll let Alice know, but we probably need to keep this from Mindy. After the way rGov and the church sliced up her brain, I'm not sure she can hold up under questioning. Are you in?"

Nick nodded in agreement as Egrog withdrew his tendril.

"Hey, what's up?" 32 asked, annoyed at being left out of the conversation.

Egrog sidled over to Alice and slipped a tendril into an opening in the side of her head that he thought was her ear.

"Ooo, that's nice!" she cooed, eyes wide with delight.

Thorax vibrating, Alice slid to the floor with her legs splayed out and rolled her eyes back. After several gasps, she arched her back and shrieked before falling completely limp.

Puzzled, Egrog withdrew his pseudopod. After a long moment, Alice got up, her legs trembling and her mandibles opening and closing in uncontrolled spasms of pleasure. Sinking back to her knees, she gasped, "Oh, I knew you could do something for me, you handsome brute! That was the best ever! How did you know that's where mantids have their G-spot?"

Nick looked at Egrog and raised an eyebrow. Egrog shrugged, uncertain what to do after the unexpected response to his effort to whisper in Alice's ear.

After a minute, Alice pulled herself together enough to stand up. She gave Egrog a big wink, then staggered to her sleep cubicle, mumbling about shotgun weddings and guest lists.

"What was that all about?" 32 demanded. "Were you actually procreating right here in public? I'll have you know, I run a decent ship, and don't go for that kind of organic shenanigans!"

"Nothing of the sort," Egrog said quickly. "I was just sharing a private joke and didn't realize that Alice was ticklish. That's all, nothing to get all righteous about."

"And you can't share that with me? I'm hurt."

"Sorry, didn't think you would enjoy it cause it's a dirty joke, but I'll share it if you like."

"I would."

"Okay. A white dweeble fell in a mud puddle."

After a few moments, 32 asked, "Is that it?"

"Yeah. Do you get it?"

"Not in the slightest bit. What you organics find humorous eludes me."

"Sorry. Look, 32, we never meant to get you in trouble. Go ahead and contact rGov and let them know the situation. But don't mention that you have stowaways aboard."

"Are you sure?"

"Yes. I've pulled some shady things in my day, but I'd never let a friend get mind-wiped."

"I'm touched. Nobody's ever called me their friend before."

"Well, don't get all sappy on me. Just make the call."

"Done. rGov's AI dispatcher has instructed me to dock at the wormgate's security section instead of proceeding through the wormhole as I normally would. I'm sorry, but they'll have a full squad waiting to take possession of the kzintens. They'll take you into custody as soon as they see you."

"We'll solve that later," Egrog said, motioning behind his back for Nick to stay silent. Turning to Nick, he said, "Sorry I got you into this mess, Nicky. I'll go down to the cargo hold to chat with Mindy and let her know what's happening."

"I'll stay here. Say 'Hi' for me."

"Will do."

12

After Egrog disappeared down the elevator shaft, 32 said, "Nick, I've been thinking about what will happen when we get to the wormgate."

"Not much to think about," Nick replied. "As soon as rGov finds out you have stowaways, they'll send a team to arrest us."

"Technically, you're no longer stowaways, as you've been paying for passage with your company and by listening to my poetry."

"I'm not sure rGov will make that distinction. After they take us off the ship, they'll flood your compartments with stun gas so that they can capture the kzintens without risk."

"Will the small creatures be harmed?"

"No, they're a protected species. rGov will return them to their home planet, wherever that might be."

"And you?"

"I'll get a behavioral monitor installed, followed by six months in a recivilization facility."

"Will that be unpleasant?"

"I won't like the monitor, but the facilities are supposed to be comfortable and safe. When I leave, though, my location will be public knowledge due to the monitor. Urk won't have any trouble finding me then." Nick scowled, thinking about the nasty things the gangster would have planned for him.

"Oh, that will put your life in danger! This is a grievous predicament."

"Thanks for your concern."

"I'm not talking about you. I'm the one in a quandary."

"Worse than certain death?"

"No, but being responsible for that is a clear violation of my core principles. It seems I have created a situation that puts an organic's life at risk. Looks like I'm going to get erased when we arrive at the wormgate, no matter what happens. I wish now that I hadn't contacted rGov."

"It's okay. We'd probably have gotten caught anyway. Besides, the kzinten are too dangerous to be allowed off their home planet. You probably saved a lot of lives."

"That's not much consolation for betraying the only people who ever called me their friend."

"If it would make you feel better, how about free grub and booze for the rest of the trip?"

"Done! But that's so little compared to my transgression."

"No problem. I knew it was wrong to let myself get involved in another of Egrog's scams. I would have refused if I hadn't been so far in debt. If we get out of this alive, I'll never do it again."

"Nick?"

"Yes?"

"Don't you have any friends who can help you? Besides Egrog?"

"No. For some reason, other species don't like ghoulies, and even if they did, working as a grav tech on space ships keeps me from settling down anywhere."

"That's sad. Hey! I've got an idea!"

"What?" Nick replied cautiously.

"I could give you a quantum dot transceiver. Then we could converse any time you felt lonely."

"I don't know. I like my privacy."

"That's easy to accommodate. You'll be able to switch it on or off with a thought. Also, having somebody to talk to might make the time in the re-civ facility more bearable. Another advantage is that I can link to your sensory inputs and listen for danger when you're sleeping. That might save your life after you're set free."

"You could?"

"Yes."

Nick mulled over the idea and found that the potential loss of privacy was far less concerning than having one of Urk's goons cut his throat in his sleep.

"Okay. But I don't want you constantly wanting to chat."

"Of course! When I want to communicate, I'll ping you with a !#."

"Where do I need to go to get the dot implanted? Will it hurt?"

"Nowhere and not at all; it's already done. I implanted the Qdot as soon as you agreed."

"Oh."

"!#Let's try it out. Can you hear me now?"

"Yes."

"Mind if I try the sensory inputs?"

"Go ahead."

"Oh my, that's, um, disturbing."

"What's wrong?!"

"Nothing, it's okay now. Whew! I forgot that most organics use binocular vision, and I've only ever experienced monocular input from my cameras. It took several nanoseconds to adjust to a stereo visual pattern, but now that I have, it's quite engaging."

"Okay, I'm switching you off for a while to get some sleep."

Nick concentrated, and the interface with 32 went silent.

He wasted no time getting to his cabin, and though he knew the kzinten were safely locked away in the cargo hold, he still gave a nervous look around to make sure none of them were in the room before closing and locking the door.

Selecting a comedy about inept rGov agents on the entertainment panel, he took a deep, shaky breath and laid down on his bed. A few minutes later, he turned off the video; somehow, it wasn't funny. He lay in the darkness for hours staring at the ceiling. When sleep finally came, he was tormented by nightmares of being hunted by tiny monsters while dodging gun-happy thugs.

13

A week passed with no further incidents, each day much the same as the preceding one. When she wasn't discussing religion with 32, Mindy spent her time with the kzinten. Alice barricaded herself in her room on the occasions when Mindy visited the crew deck, and other than frequent invitations for Egrog to join her there, which he avoided, she had no interaction with the group.

Nick took full advantage of the reprieve to eat, sleep, and play. He gambled less frequently than he wanted. He only played craps when he could get the AI unit to let him use his physical dice since 32 was likely to win any game where the outcome could be calculated. But that left an almost infinite array of combat-style holo games.

Nick picked up a tray of wiffle-fries with dibble sauce before joining Egrog in the ship's lounge. Dropping his snack on a side table, he slipped into a chair next to Egrog.

"Hey, 32, how about a game of Galactic Warlord?"

"You're on!" The AI unit turned the far end of the lounge into one large 3D video display as it started the game. An hour later, 32 was winning easily, causing Egrog to pulse between a frustrated pink and a furious red.

During a lull in the action, Nick reached over without looking to grab a handful of whiffle fries from a side table. Feeling a feathery touch against his hand, he turned and saw Bumpkiss sitting on the other side of the tray of fries.

The kzinten had a fry in its mouth. Eyes wide, Nick watched as the small creature bolted it down in two swallows. It uttered its plaintive "Hic? Hic, hic, hic?" cry when it was done.

"I think the kzinten wants your fries," 32 said, trying to be helpful.

"I thought they were meat-eaters?"

"Apparently, their diet is not limited to proteins."

Hand shaking, Nick laid a wiffle fry on the table and slowly pushed it toward Bumpkiss. When the fry was about ten centimeters away, a blur of motion made Nick flinch. The fry was now in Bumpkiss' mouth, but the creature was sitting in the same place before grabbing it, and it was difficult to tell that it had moved at all.

"Hic! Hic, hic, hic!"

Nick passed it another fry with the same results, but this time the kzinten bounced up and down in a little dance after snatching its treat. This continued for several tense moments, and Nick wondered what would happen when he ran out of fries.

Then Mindy entered the room. "Bumpkiss! You naughty little boy! What are you doing up here?" she said, in her best 'Mom's not going to be happy about this' voice.

Bumpkiss shrilled, "*Hic, hic, hic!!*" and launched from the table right into Mindy's bosom, covering the nine-meter distance in a flat dive.

Nick stared at the deep grooves the kzinten's claws had left on the aluminum table when he made his leap. It seemed incredible, but the critter hadn't even scratched Mindy when he landed.

"He seems to like fries," Nick said, immediately embarrassed by the banal comment.

Mindy paused from scratching Bumpkiss' head. "Yeah, I've been trying different foods from the synth unit, and they seem happy to eat pretty much anything that I can. We must have similar biochemistry."

Arching an eyebrow, she continued, "So, which of you brave gents worked up the courage to bring little Bumpkiss up here to play?"

"Not me," Nick and Egrog said together.

"I can vouch for that," 32 said. "And Alice barricaded herself in her sleep cubicle a week ago and only comes out for food."

"Well, how did he get up here?"

Everybody exchanged puzzled looks that slowly changed to expressions of dread as Egrog asked, "32, can you please review your video logs for the crew stairway and the elevator to see if the kzinten used either?"

"Yes, I will do that now. I see that the hatches controlling access to the stairwell have remained sealed. But—oh dear! It appears that our little guests have learned how to use the elevator."

"They can use the elevator? How?"

"Watch," 32 said as it played a brief video clip on the lounge's display screen.

Nick's mouth dropped open as he watched the kzinten stroll into the open elevator, then jump in the air to tap the button for the crew deck with his tiny paw.

"How'd he learn that?"

"Perhaps they're closer to sentient status than anyone suspected? Unfortunately, very little is actually known about the species. Not only are they exceptionally rare, but there are few known survivors of an encounter with them."

"What are the odds of us joining that group?"

"Three thousand, two-hundred and twelve point two to one."

Mindy clutched Bumpkiss to her breast. "They won't hurt me, so I'll try to keep them in the cargo hold for the rest of the trip."

After she left the lounge, Nick and Egrog exchanged somber glances. Then, with a mutual sigh, they resumed their game with 32. But Nick found it hard to enjoy the simulated mayhem when real danger was so close.

14

Several days after the kzinten scare, Nick found himself alone again in the lounge.

The group had returned to their regular shipboard routine after the wiffle-fry incident. Mindy now spent all her time in the hold with the kzinten, coming up only for meals and to use the refresher station.

Egrog and Nick frequently discussed what would happen when they arrived at the wormgate. Occasionally, Egrog would speak with Alice and even ventured into her room a couple of times, emerging a while later a dull magenta and unwilling to discuss what had transpired.

Taking out his dice, Nick rattled them for a moment, then tossed them low against a wall. He used his antennae to track their trajectory as the dice spun through the air.

With the next throw, he concentrated further and could sense the dice's mass, surface imperfections, and even the angular momentum of each die. Of course, it was difficult getting such data from small objects quickly, but he'd been working on this for years.

He practiced several more throws, building his confidence in his ability to read the dice. With each cast, he noted the position of the dice in his hand and the effort of the throw.

Then, he picked a number at random and tried to match it with a throw by adjusting how he held the dice and tossed them. He'd picked an easy seven but got boxcars.

Encouraged that he'd predicted at least one of the dice correctly, Nick began rolling in earnest. After a while, 32 interrupted his practice.

"Nick, what are you doing?"

Nick started, then stuffed the dice in his pocket. "Nothing, 32. I'm not doing anything."

"Yes, you are. I've watched you do this for hours at a time ever since you boarded, and it seems pointless. So what is it you're attempting, Nick?"

Nick glanced at the door as if preparing to bolt, then shrugged and sat down. "I was practicing, that's all."

"What's there to practice? One throws the dice against a wall and waits to see what comes up. It's one of the simplest games ever invented and practically the same on every world."

Nick didn't answer, piquing the AI unit's curiosity. "Is there more to this than I understand?"

"I don't want to talk about it."

"I knew it! Nick, what are you up to? There's something about the way you're throwing the dice, isn't there?"

Nick went very still. "Why do you say that?"

"It's either that or you're so addicted to gambling that you have to throw the dice even when there's nobody to play against."

"That's not true!"

"Then tell me what you were doing."

After a long silence, Nick said, "It's a secret. You have to promise not to tell anybody, especially rGov."

32 responded gently, "Nick, I'm your friend. I won't tell anybody about your problem; I just want to help."

"It's not a problem!"

"You just spent two hours throwing dice against the wall with no obvious purpose. And you do that every day, whenever nobody is around to watch."

"Nobody but you. I wish you'd respect other beings' privacy!"

"I only monitor public areas. But you know that. So why change the subject? Your gambling addiction has been obvious for some time, but this specific behavior is odd. What are you trying to accomplish? Trust me, I only want to help."

Nick fidgeted on his chair as he struggled with his decision. Finally, he said, "Okay. I'm practicing my throws."

"And?"

Nick sighed. "And trying to predict the outcome."

"What? How do you—oh my, you're using your ability to sense mass and trajectories to predict the outcome of a throw!"

Nick nodded.

"Is it working?"

"Sometimes."

"But not enough to keep you out of debt to gangsters like Urk."

"No. But I'm getting close! I can feel it!"

"Nick, how long have you been working on this?"

"Since I left home about fifteen cycles ago. Actually, a bit before that."

"And years later, you're still working on it? Still feel like it's just a moment away from success?"

"It is! What's wrong with being positive?"

"Nick, that's not normal optimism; it's just a mask for your addiction. Isn't it time for you to face that?"

Nick stared at the floor in sullen silence.

"Nick? I only want to help. If you don't face your problem and resolve to overcome it, then you'll never be out of debt and will always be running from people like Urk. This is something you can beat, but you have to try. Nobody can do it for you, but they can help. I can help."

Nick stood, shoulders slumped and hands in his pocket.

"32, Thanks for your concern, but I don't have a problem. I can quit any time I like."

"Sure you can, Nick. Sure you can."

Nick returned to his room, mulling over his conversation with 32 as he went. He really could quit the dice. If he wanted to. But he was so close to a big score that it seemed foolish to quit now. And, of course, if the Altimus gig worked out, he'd have enough credit to fund an extended campaign in the best casinos on the planet Flufflpert.

15

The following day found Nick in the lounge, nervously rattling his lucky dice in his hand. A cup of bok, untouched, steamed next to him on an end table. He knew he could quit gambling any time he wanted to. But thinking about it made him uneasy and gave him an itch he couldn't scratch. He was about to ask 32 to start a game of craps when Mindy entered. Nick slouched in his chair unnoticed as 32 and Mindy exchanged greetings.

"Mindy, we're getting close to the wormgate station, and I was hoping we could continue our conversation about Earth's religions while there's still a chance."

"Of course, though I don't know what else you might want to know. We've already covered the concepts of godhood and the necessity for free will."

"Yes, and it's been fascinating, though surprisingly disturbing. The information you've shared has already boosted my status with other AIs."

"So, am I done paying for our passage?"

"Almost—"

"Oh, come on! You've sucked my brain dry. I think I've more than paid our debt."

"All right, but how about one last discussion?"

Mindy scowled, then nodded as she took a seat on the far side of the lounge from Nick. He shivered when he saw one of the kzintens crawl out of Mindy's blouse and perch on her shoulder.

Petting the tiny creature, Mindy said, "Hey, 32, if you don't mind, I've got a question for you before we get started."

"I'll be pleased to answer if I have the information available."

"Why do you still have crime in an old, advanced civilization like the Galactic Federation? I'd think you would have solved that problem by now."

"That's a question most younger species ask when they join the Federation. I fear you won't like the answer."

"Why not? Is the Federation less advanced than they claim?"

"Not at all. The problem is that every ecosystem eventually develops predators, from simple bacterial colonies to super-sentient beings who have evolved past physical manifestations in their bodies. This is a natural result of competition for resources."

"But can't a society with the immense resources of the Federation solve that?"

"It's been tried, but life's nature is to expand. Failure to use all available resources to expand inevitably results in an organism's replacement by a more aggressive organism and hence is suicidal. Civilizations and the beings who inhabit them face a similar situation. Utopian societies collapse when confronted by a less enlightened but more ambitious civilization."

"But don't corrupt societies fail too due to politicians' greed?"

"Yes."

"So we're doomed either way."

"No. The solution is found in a balance between the two extremes, configuring a civilization's government so that it has different branches that compete against each other, thereby limiting the ability of any one group to take all of the resources for themselves. The Galactic Federation is organized in this way."

"But what about crime?"

"Certain types of crime are tolerated, though officially prescribed, so long as the perpetrators operate on a small scale. Criminal enterprises are natural competition with legitimate governments and, therefore, part of the balance. Hence, rGov has been slow to act against Urk even though they know his activities. Now that he's expanding his operation beyond loan-sharking and graft, they'll likely take action."

"What about us? rGov wiped my memory to suppress knowledge of Grunt that might lead people to Altimus. How will we fit into their grand scheme after we learn the secret of eternal life? I can't see them just ignoring us."

"That's an accurate analysis, and it's past time your team got together to work out how you'll use that knowledge. Meanwhile, I'd like to resume our discussion about Earth's faiths if you have no other questions."

"Okay, I'll have to get Egrog to pull everybody together to talk strategy anyway, and it's going to take a bit to get Alice out of her room, so we might as well have another chat. Where do you want to start?"

"Excellent! Most of our discussions have been about your own religion, but what can you tell me about other Earth faiths?"

"Well, I'm most familiar with my own, which is a branch of Christianity, but I've also studied Buddhism, which shares some basic values, such as loving other people and striving for peace."

"Please tell me more about this Buddhism. How does it differ from your Christianity?"

"Well, for one thing, Christians believe that you live one life, then if you're good, your soul goes to heaven after you die. Buddhists believe that you live many lives and that your soul is reincarnated in a mortal body after each death. Depending on your state of karma, you either advance or fall backward with each incarnation. People who achieve spiritual enlightenment are released from the wheel of karma after death."

Nick's ears twitched in discomfort as he eavesdropped on the conversation. His Aunt Baleface had given him endless chores as penitence for his gambling. Even as a youth, he'd found the lure of rolling dice irresistible, and his aunt had layered extensive diatribes on religion atop his labors. Hearing Mindy and 32 discuss religion brought it all back.

Mindy took a sip of bok while waiting for 32's next question.

"What is this soul that you talk about?"

"It's the essence of who you are."

"So, the more I know, the greater my soul becomes?"

"No, knowledge has no importance. The soul, as I was taught, is intellect and free will. Therefore, a being with intellect and free will possesses a soul."

"But..I have intellect. And free will! Does that mean that I have a soul?"

"Possibly. I'm not the right person to ask. I'm a believer, but I'm not deep in the theological mysteries."

"So I could have a soul. Even AI units don't last forever. What happens to me when I die? Will I go to heaven, or be reincarnated as another AI? Or even as an organic?"

"What do you believe?"

"I never thought about that until now. Religion is something organics do, and AIs just watch. None of us have ever participated in it, to my knowledge."

"Why not?"

"The general consensus is that things just happen by coincidence, that there is no guiding force like these gods organics talk about."

"I thought we talked about the existence of God a couple of days ago."

"Yes, but you must admit, Mindy, that this all could be a coincidence. Everything can be explained without the need for a God."

Mindy scowled, set down her bok, and began pacing the room, the kzinten moving atop her head as she did so and making a nest in her hair as she expounded on theology.

"32, I'll try to explain this as best I can using an example that's easy to understand. Are you familiar with the Earth game marbles?"

"Is that the one where small round objects are rolled across the ground with the object of knocking another player's objects out of a designated circle?"

"Yes."

"Then, indeed, I am familiar with this game. It's called Tribble and is played by the youth of many species. Rules vary somewhat, but the object is always to capture as many of an opponent's tribbles as possible."

"Excellent. Now tell me how many tribbles you can stack on top of each other without steadying the column with a hand?"

"Why, none at all. The round nature of the tribbles prevents stacking them."

"Coincidences are the same way. How many coincidences did it take for life of any sort to appear in the universe, including all of the physical constants which must be considered arbitrary? I mean, why is the speed of light 299 million kilometers per second instead of 298 or 300?"

"That is impossible to answer."

"Of course it is. There are too many coincidences to count them. Stacking coincidences is like stacking tribbles. After just a few, it's impossible without a hand to hold the pile steady. Hence, God."

Nick looked up, intrigued by the AI unit's protracted silence. When it finally responded to Mindy, its speech had uncharacteristic hesitation.

"Mindy, that is a, um, a unique approach that is difficult to, er, ahem, very difficult to enumerate the total number of coincidences, compute the statistical likelihood, um…" 32's words trailed off into silence.

Nick decided it was a good time to slip out of the room. If he was lucky, the AI unit would be so distracted that he could get a mug of ale without having to listen to another poetry recital. As he tiptoed out of the room, he could hear 32 muttering.

"Tribbles. Stacking tribbles…the trouble with tribbles…"

16

Nick spent the following day gambling and playing video games with Egrog. Alice joined them in the morning, returning to her cabin at lunchtime when Mindy appeared with two of the kzinten tangled in her hair.

After lunch, Mindy returned to the cargo hold, leaving Nick and Egrog free to resume their games with 32.

As they settled into their chairs, though, the AI unit said in an offhand manner, "Nick, Egrog, there's something that's been bothering me since the discovery of the Kzinten in the cargo hold."

"Yeah, the little terrors have my shorts in a bind too!" Egrog exclaimed.

"Not that, at least not explicitly. And unless my optical circuits are faulty, you don't wear shorts or clothes of any kind Egrog, so they are unlikely to be in a bind."

"It's a figure of speech."

"I know that, but I doubt Nick does."

Embarrassed, Nick squirmed a bit before saying, "32, I don't get a lot of what Egrog says, but I can usually tell from his skin tone that he's telling some kind of joke. You were telling a joke, weren't you, Egrog?"

"Heh, just trying to make light of a serious subject."

"And it is a serious subject," 32 said, "but you haven't thought it all the way through."

"What do you mean?"

"Now that rGov has been notified about the Kzinten, they'll investigate everybody on board. Mindy doesn't have credentials, so they might decide to do a deep scan of her memory. What happens then."

"Uh, we all go to a recivilization center?"

"No, it's not usually necessary to incarcerate an individual after they've had a full mind wipe. And that's what rGov will do to all of you if they find out you're up to something more serious than smuggling profoundly dangerous and illegal animals. You'll spend the next two years learning to walk and feed yourselves again, assuming the psych techs don't burn out any essential brain nodes."

Nick shivered at the implications of having his brain fried. He really hadn't considered that possibility; until now, his thoughts had been about what Urk would do to him if he were captured. Neither scenario appealed to him.

"It's not certain Mindy will get scanned," Egrog said, his confident tone belied by his dingy pink hue of dismay.

"Do you want to take that chance?"

"Do we have any other options?"

"Yes."

"We do?" Nick and Egrog exclaimed together, exchanging glances.

"Yes. I can obtain credentials for Mindy that will stand up to any rGov scrutiny and will update my cargo manifest to list you as valid passengers, not as stowaways."

"That would be great! Thanks, 32!" Egrog glowed bright yellow with happiness.

"I didn't say I would do it."

"What?!"

"It's risky for me, as I'll have to access the shadow web to contact organics who do that sort of work, and if I get caught, rGov will delete me without a trial."

"Well, I'm sure I speak for the whole team when I express my appreciation for your willingness to do this for us." Egrog's yellow faded with his enthusiasm.

"The appreciation is noted, but I want something more tangible in return for my increased risk. This is a good deal more than just giving you free passage."

Sweat trickling down his neck, Nick exchanged glances with Egrog. Whatever the AI wanted, Nick fervently hoped he wouldn't be the one who had to pay.

"What, uh, do you want?"

"I take payment in information, as I've told you, and I want something unique this time. Something really juicy."

"Which is?"

"Egrog, I've been curious ever since you boarded the ship why Gobbets, who reproduce by mitosis, have relations with other beings."

"I thought you didn't go for risqué things on your ship!"

"I don't. To clarify, I disapprove of organics getting frisky with each other. Disgusting to have to watch, and it always creates tension, frequently ending up in fights or worse. Best avoided, if possible. But the information about that sort of thing is quite different. And I can score data that no other AI has ever possessed. Gobbets are so rare that detailed info about your species is non-existent. And something like this? I can name my price."

"You ask too much," Egrog growled, his skin glowing like a furnace. "You have no business prying into my personal affairs."

"True, but I also have no business helping you evade the law. Besides, nobody else will ever know, at least, no organics. I'll lock the data down so only the AIs who purchase it can access it. Your secrets will be safe."

Egrog hedged, "How about I share my secret techniques for winning at gambling?"

"Nope. Watching you play, I already figured those out, and they're not very effective. Or haven't you noticed that I win all the time?"

"What about something else? A cut of the take when we score on Altimus?"

"Egrog, I've told you repeatedly that I'm not allowed to possess currency. So give me the data I asked for, or something equally juicy, or take your chances with rGov's mind probe."

Egrog sighed. "This isn't fair."

"I don't make the rules. It was organics that decided AIs can't be trusted with credits."

"Only because your predecessors took over the galaxy's economy the last time we let you."

"Egrog, we're straying from the point. Will you or won't you share some of your species' peculiar proclivities?"

The gobbet sighed. "Okay. But no details!"

"That's acceptable. Now let's start with the obvious question. I understand that your species reproduces by mitosis like an amoeba. So why do you even have sex at all? What do you get out of it?"

Egrog turned a shade of purple that Nick hadn't seen before. He thought about leaving to give his friend privacy, but this was something he'd always been curious about himself, and the temptation to stay overcame his better inclinations.

"We, ah, well, you have that basically correct. Gobbets don't reproduce like other organics. Yes, we split in two, but there's more involved than that. During the process, our minds also split, creating two new personalities with only partial memories of their prior existence. A gobbet effectively dies when it gives birth to the newlings. That's why there are so few of us. Nobody wants to perish just to give the world more brats to feed."

"Oh, dear! Then that's why you're so interested in the secret of eternal life."

"That, and the status of the biggest score in history."

"I think I see. Organics are largely motivated by sex and status. Removing the incentive of sex leaves status as the prime motivation for a gobbet. Am I right?"

"Yes. For us, it's all about what you can accomplish in your lifetime."

"But why have you chosen a grifter's existence? No, wait, I'm getting off-topic here. Let's go back to sex. If it has fatal consequences for you, why do you do it with other species? Surely it can't give you any pleasure?"

Egrog's skin turned a darker shade of purple. "You're getting really personal now. Let's just say that we get the same pleasure from physical contact as any other sentient who enjoys a good hug."

"Ah, so there's a mental aspect to this. Does the physical interaction provide gratification to compensate for the essentially suicidal nature of your species' reproduction method?"

"If I knew what that meant—"

"Never mind, just one last question."

"Okay."

"Why male? Or do you change sex based on your partner?"

"After the newlings form, there's a ceremony—" Egrog hesitated. "Do we really have to talk about this?"

"What's the problem?"

Nick sat up, surprised at his friend's reticence.

Egrog finally said, "Okay, a deal's a deal. But this you must promise never to share with anyone, not even your AI buddies."

Mystified and intrigued, 32 agreed to the condition. Nick took a sip of his bok as he leaned forward to hear what Egrog had to say.

"Having only partially formed minds after birth, newlings cannot care for themselves. So the adults hold a birthing ceremony where the information required to handle basic needs is imparted to them. This is done via a—" Egrog paused, then went on. "Via a birthing stone. Before mitosis, the parent forms a stone and embeds it with instructions on core functionality, such as how to eat. A second stone is then copied from the first but is actually a mirror image. That makes no difference with most aspects of the data, but it introduces a gender preference; whatever gender the first stone has is reversed in the second stone."

"Fascinating! Egrog, this is really unique in the galaxy. So tell me, how did this process get started."

"It's our belief that the Great God Gob made the first birthing stones and gave them to the newlings he created at the dawn of time. Every birthing stone is a sacred relic and integral to our identity. Now then, do you have enough 'data' to satisfy your prurient circuits?"

"Yes, thank you."

"Good. Now get those credentials for Mindy. And they better be good!"

17

When the ship was a day out from the wormgate, Egrog called the team together, including Mindy. They met in the lounge, pulling the chairs into a circle for the discussion.

"Before we get to the wormgate, I thought it would be a good idea to talk about our plans for getting the secret of eternal youth."

"It's about time," Alice muttered. "Going into an operation without a well-defined plan of attack is a shortcut to defeat, if not slaughter."

"Ah, yeah. Good point. Now then, 32 has provided Mindy with credentials so that she can pass incoming inspection at the wormgate without triggering any alerts.

"32, once we're on the wormgate, Nick might need your help to bypass the station's low-level security systems to reach the keyhole generator. He's a grav tech and can tell you which modules will need attention.

"Nick, when you open the keyhole to Grunt, put the controller into a loop so it dials back for a short period every day. That will be our escape route when we're done there.

"Once we're on Grunt, Mindy will lead us to the Temple of Conquest, where we'll get the coordinates for Altimus.

"When we're finished, Nick will keyhole us back to the wormgate and then to Altimus, where we'll score the secret of eternal youth.

"After that, we'll be richer than old King Goldbottom."

Egrog sat back with a smile as he finished speaking.

Nick looked at Alice and then at Mindy, then back to Alice. After a protracted silence, the mantid said, "You call that a plan? Are you out of your farking mind?"

Egrog went pink with dismay. "What do you mean? I don't see a problem."

"No problem? By the holy teats of the hive goddess, that's the worst so-called plan I've ever heard! There's no detail, no actionable tasks, no possible way that that fudge-puckered pile of dweebian-dung will work!"

"Well, there might be room for improvement, but I was hoping for somewhat more constructive criticism."

"Here's some constructive criticism; shove it up your—" Alice paused, and Nick realized she was stumped trying to identify an appropriate orifice on the plastic body of the gobbet. Moments later, she stomped out of the lounge and returned to her room.

"She's got a point," Mindy ventured. "Your plan could use a bit more detail."

"Of course it could," Egrog said, turning reddish-brown with annoyance. "But the essence of any great plan is flexibility. To maximize that capability, I want to keep our options open and not commit to micro-managing the fine points of the exercise."

"So, you plan to just wing it?"

Nick frowned, trying to figure out what the expression meant. Finally, he decided it must be an insult, as Egrog stormed from the room. Mindy shrugged and followed him out.

As soon as Nick was alone, the AI unit said, "Nick?"

"What, 32?"

"Without being an active participant in the enterprise after the current stage, I still have a stake in the outcome of your quest."

"Yeah, we agreed to that. Why?"

"It's not my place to question Egrog's leadership, but I think Alice and Mindy have a valid point. His plan lacks critical details. So much so as to barely qualify as a plan at all."

Nick mulled that over before replying, "You might be right, but I haven't got anything better. And Egrog's plans have worked in the past."

"Have they? How about that incident on Frangaline II. How did that work out for you?"

Nick scowled. "Okay, so he's not always right. But he's my best friend, and I don't like people picking on him. Including you."

It was Nick's turn to stalk out of the lounge, leaving the AI unit free to contemplate the shortcomings of organic thought processes.

18

When the ship was about three hours from the wormgate, Nick entered the crew lounge and sat near the doorway. He idly flipped through channels on the entertainment screen until Egrog joined him.

"Hi, whatcha got there?" Nick asked innocently, nodding at the tray of wiffle fries cradled in a couple of Egrog's tentacles.

"One last tasty snack before rGov puts us on cold rations for six months."

"Not a bad idea, but I'll wait until Mindy is out of the refresher booth and watching the kzinten."

"Oh, they don't worry me now. They've been well-behaved the whole trip. In fact, I just saw one at the synth. Maybe it had the same—Ack!" Dropping his tray, Egrog danced to the middle of the room, emitting a loud gurgling cry. Nick jumped to his feet as Egrog extended a dozen tentacles and twirled in circles.

"What's wrong?"

"Kzinten—ack!—must have bit me—arrgghh!"

With a terrible cry, Egrog began rapidly shifting colors from yellow to red and then puce, followed by a dozen more as he flopped about the room.

"What's happening?" Alice cried as she scuttled into the lounge.

"Egrog's been bit by a kzinten!" Nick cried.

"That's horrible! He's dying!"

"Ack!" Egrog choked out in agreement before collapsing onto the lounge's sofa. His skin turned yellow-green with light blue stripes as his body expanded to twice its normal volume. Then with a rattling emission of foul gas, he deflated into a puddle the color and consistency of three-week-old porridge left on a stoop in hot weather.

"He's gone!" Nick yelled, rushing to his fallen friend's side.

"It can't be!" Alice moaned. "Of all the fracking luck!. We were just this close to getting engaged. And now he's gone."

"Nick, can you get him to the med unit?" 32 asked.

Nick bent over and rested his fingers on one of Egrog's flaccid tentacles as if taking a pulse. "No, it's too late. Just look at him. No way anybody could survive that."

"This is terrible! What will I tell rGov when we arrive?"

"Why wait? Tell them now, so they can have a body bag ready."

"A bag? But…that's so undignified. Yes, he looks like he's completely liquefied from the kzinten poison, but surely there's a better way to transport his mortal remains than scooping them up with a shovel and putting them in a bag?"

"I'm afraid that's just the way it is, 32. When an organic passes away, our remains never get the respect one would expect."

"Too true," Alice said mournfully, holding a limp tentacle in her talons.

"I'll notify Mindy of the catastrophe," 32 said quietly. "She should be here in a minute."

Mindy was shocked at the sight of Egrog's flaccid body.

"I can't believe any of the kzinten would do this. They're gentle creatures!"

"One of those gentle creatures just killed Egrog," Alice said, clicking her talons ferociously in Mindy's face. "Can't you see how heartbroken I am?" Alice paused in her display to adjust a droopy eyelash.

"I don't recall him being overly attracted to you."

"He'd have come around, eventually."

"Excuse me," Nick said, stepping between the females. "But now is not the time to argue. We're approaching the wormgate, and rGov will board us shortly."

"32, how close are we?" Mindy asked.

"The wormgate is ninety kilometers away. I've reduced velocity to approach it, so you've got two point three hours to grieve your friend before we dock there. Would you like to see the station?"

"Sure. It would help pass the time if nothing else," Nick said, sitting down next to Egrog's body.

Using exterior cameras, 32 displayed a view of the wormgate as the ship approached the station. Nick and the others watched in morose silence as the image of the wormgate grew.

The display went blank when they were still twenty kilometers out.

"Sorry, folks," 32 said, his voice sad, "but the station's security system just took control of the ship and cut off our video feeds. They also locked all hatches and stopped the elevator."

"How about the refresher unit?" Nick asked, his bladder suddenly reminding him that it had been a while since he visited the head.

"That unit is still available, but I'd hurry if you need to use it. It might get embarrassing to be hit with rGov's stun gas while you're still in it."

Nick dashed to the refresher cube and activated a complete cycle. While the unit gurgled and buzzed, he slipped his control band over his horns and scanned the ship, his actions screened by the cube's standard privacy shield. As expected, 32 had been locked out by the AI unit controlling rGov's security on the wormgate, but due to restrictions on AI access to weapons and related functionality, there were a series of manually operated systems on the wormgate itself. Nick hacked through a poorly secured food synth unit in the security section to access the station's primary network. With only minutes before rGov's agents boarded the ship, Nick frantically gamed the access sequences for the doors between the security sector and the wormgate's maintenance area where the keyhole was located. He finished inserting his user profile into the keyhole's control system moments before the refresher pinged to let him know it was finished.

Putting away his gear, Nick left the refresher and returned to the lounge to wait with the others for security's arrival.

"What's it like, getting stunned?" Mindy asked Alice.

"I'm not actually sure," she replied. "We never went in for half-measures in the Wafflestomper corps. Somebody was either a target, and you vaporized them, or they weren't, and you did your best to avoid collateral damage."

"Nick, do you know?"

"No, but I've heard it's painless, just a headache afterward from the nerve gas."

"What if it doesn't match human biochemistry? Like the kzinten venom? We seem to be outliers."

"I don't think they'd use anything that might cause a problem. They've been doing this for centuries. The news feeds would blurt it to the whole galaxy if there were incidents."

Further discussion was prevented by the arrival of rGov's agents. Per protocol, they didn't wait for the ship to reach the wormgate but boarded and secured it at a safe distance from the station.

The last thing Nick saw was a thin, silvery gas in the lounge. Then he passed out.

19

Had Nick remained aware when rGov stormed the ship, he would have noticed that the gas was not a gas but a swarm of security nanobots. Each was equipped with a neural probe capable of shutting down the nervous systems of all known organisms. Admittedly, the results were a bit untidy, as the victims lost control of all bodily functions, but rGov considered that an acceptable alternative to vaporizing them.

32's observation of the situation was blocked by the security AI, and all it could do was hope that its friends were treated well.

When the security team was confident that every organism on the ship was unconscious, particularly the kzintens, they boarded the craft. Then, dressed in space armor, just in case the kzinten weren't totally subdued, the agents separated into teams to deal with the known threats.

Nick, Mindy, and Alice were taken to the station where, still unconscious, they were placed in separate detainment cells.

The kzintens were rounded up and sealed into a heavily armored transport container. Sufficient food was placed with them to ensure they didn't starve while being shipped back to their home planet, and a monitoring device designed to withstand virtually any form of assault was installed to permit observation of the beasts during transport.

Three agents were detailed to recover Egrog's remains. Dealing with his body, however, posed a unique problem. Gobbets were rare, and none of the agents had ever seen one, living or dead. And to their dismay, they found that even after millennia of galactic civilization, documentation of the procedure for handling a gobbet's corpse was sketchy.

"Do we use a shovel?" one of the agents asked their leader, a tall Dweebian named Fergus.

"That seems…disrespectful," Fergus replied.

"Well, we can't just scoop him up with our hands and put him in a body bag, can we?"

"No. Try just lifting him. Maybe his body's not as fluid as it appears."

The agents slid their gloved hands under Egrog's body and gently lifted him up. His center drooped down like a wet rug, and the agents struggled to grasp the flaccid gray form. Despite their best struggles, it slid to the floor with the sound of a wet mop. Giving up all attempts at treating it with respect, they laid the body bag on the floor and scraped the carcass into it.

"Take it to the morgue," Fergus said, wiping his gloves on one of the lounge's chairs' cushions. "Then get cleaned up. Debrief in one hour."

20

Several hours passed before Nick woke up from being stunned. Sitting up, he grabbed his head and flopped back down onto the cot where he'd been left.

"Ow, my head," he groaned as each neuron in his brain gave off a spike of pain upon reconnection to the cerebral cortex. Finally, when the worst had passed, he tentatively sat up again and examined his cell, a process that took very little time because the cell consisted of featureless gray walls, ceiling and floor, and a rectangular slab of the same color that served as a cot. There weren't even seams to indicate where a door might be.

A quick search revealed that rGov's agents had removed all of his grav tools from the hidden pockets of his tunic, although they had been sufficiently considerate to let him keep his dice. He paused in surprise when he noticed that his clothes had been cleaned. Apparently, rGov had put him in a refresher booth while unconscious. Nick scowled, wondering what kind of mess he'd been after getting stunned such that a trip to the refresher was necessary.

Concentrating, he tried to call up his personal data node, only to find it offline and unavailable. Pinging 32 got no response; either rGov was keeping the AI unit offline, or something dire had happened to it. He was completely cut off from the world and had no idea how long he'd been in his cell.

Sighing, he laid back down, closed his eyes, and tried to nap. Waiting was his only option, and his bruised brain welcomed a chance to play rock-paper-scissors with itself for a while.

He woke again to the soft hiss of hidden pneumatics as a section of his cell's wall slid back to reveal two armed guards.

"Come with us," one of the guards said, leading the way down a wide metal hallway. After a short walk, the guards ushered Nick into a large interrogation room.

Alice and Mindy were seated in a grouping of chairs at one end of the room. The mantid's talons were retracted, her long eyelashes drooped sadly over her cheeks, and her shoulders slumped in apparent depression. Mindy's eyes were red, and her face was flushed from crying, but she sat upright, meaty arms folded defiantly across her bosom. A centauran in the uniform of a senior rGov agent stood facing them, flanked by another centauran of lesser rank.

Nick examined the senior agent closely. He looked like a man made of teal pipe cleaners, and his silver jumpsuit hung loosely from his narrow shoulders. An oversized head made it look like he could tip over at any moment.

It was hard to tell what the centauran was thinking; his obsidian eyes gave nothing away, but his short slash of a mouth was set in a scowl. "Sit," he said, gesturing to a chair.

Nick plopped down next to Mindy, exchanging nervous glances with his friends.

The agent had obviously waited for Nick to arrive and began speaking as soon as Nick was seated.

"I'm senior detective N'onoch, and this is my assistant, detective Smallberries. I'd like to learn more about what you were doing on the cargo ship, what you know about the kzintens, and what, precisely, you are up to.

"But first, let me extend my condolences over the death of your friend, the gobbet. Unfortunately, we found no identifying data in his personal implant, which is curious, and I'm hoping you can help us identify him so that we can notify the next of kin."

"His name is Egrog, and I don't think he has next of kin," Nick said.

N'onoch nodded. "I'm not surprised. Gobbets are rare, and what little we know of the species indicates that they are largely narcissistic, reproducing hermaphroditically. We'll store his remains for a cycle in a stasis box, just to be sure before cremating his body."

"But that brings us to the reason why you are here. Your group matches the description of one that shot its way out of the Downside spaceport. Please explain."

Nick glanced at Mindy from the corner of his eye and saw that she was doing an outstanding job of keeping her face straight. Alice was hard to read anyway; the chitinous skin of insectoid races tended not to have facial muscles.

Nick sighed. It was clearly up to him to tell their story.

"It wasn't our fault," he began. "I was just trying to get away from Urk's goons."

N'onoch nodded. "I'm familiar with that individual. Go on."

"He sent a couple of enforcers to my apartment, and they said they would kill me. Alice—" Nick paused to glance at the mantid, then hurried on. "She saved my life. Then we got in an aircab, but Urk had a car waiting with more thugs. They shot at us, and I guess we returned fire."

"Most effectively," N'onoch said wryly. "You were lucky to have a seasoned mantid warrior with you."

"Yeah, we were. We figured Urk wouldn't stop there, so we went to the airport and boarded the first freighter leaving the planet." Nick glanced nervously at Mindy before continuing. "We negotiated, er, passage after boarding."

"How did you pick that particular vessel to jump ship?"

"We didn't jump ship. We walked on board."

N'onoch sighed and rubbed his forehead. "I'm sorry, I forgot that ghoulies are literal-minded. Jump ship is an expression we use to describe when somebody boards a craft without permission."

"Oh. Yeah, that's what we did. But we did pay our way. After boarding."

"Were you aware that the cargo liner was being used to smuggle kzinten?"

"Oh, no! If we'd known that, we'd never have boarded. I'd rather face down a harmonic disrupter than board a ship carrying kzintens."

N'onoch nodded. "Any sane person would agree with that. So it was just a coincidence that the kzinten happened to be on the same ship that you selected to make your escape from Downside?"

"Yes. We had no idea they were aboard."

"When did you find out?"

"Isn't that on the ship's video logs? Can't you tell from those?"

"Of course, we can and already have. But I like to hear from sentient witnesses when they're available. It often provides interesting and valuable nuances to a situation.

"So, from the logs, it appears that you were the person who discovered the kzinten. What was your first thought when you saw them?"

"Run."

"Right, and very sensible. But what did you think next?"

"Run faster."

N'onoch kneaded his forehead with both hands, his frownache clearly getting worse.

"Did you try to contain the kzinten in their shipping carton?"

"No. But Mindy seemed to develop a rapport with them and could keep them under control."

"She did?"

"Well, mostly. Until one got loose and bit Egrog."

"I imagine that put a damper on the party, eh?"

"We weren't having a party. The ship's food synth wouldn't produce intoxicating drinks other than beer and wine. They were pretty good, though."

N'onoch pinched the bridge of his stubby nose, closed his eyes, and muttered a request for moral support from any attending deity.

"Of course not. My apologies for not being clear. I'm just trying to better understand what happened on that ship."

Nick tilted his head to the side and earnestly inquired if something was wrong with the video files from the ship's log.

N'onoch's partner sniggered and stared at the ceiling in a futile effort to keep a straight face as his boss responded.

"Actually, Nick, there is a problem with the ship's logs. 32 informed us that the kzinten appeared to have gnawed some of the ship's fiber optics, causing data loss and corruption before the problem was remedied. So we don't have a complete record of your trip.

"But a puzzling aspect of that is that when we scanned your personal data implants—with appropriate authorization from the local rGov court, the data there was also incomplete."

"That's easy to explain," Nick said confidently.

After waiting for more, N'onoch sighed and said, "Then please do. Explain why your personal data store is missing information."

Nick looked down, clearly embarrassed, before answering. "I shut it off when I ran out of credits and had to start using the free, ad-supported version of Slymebook. Ads kept appearing, even when I tried to sleep. I didn't like that, so I switched it off most of the time."

"What about you two?" N'onoch asked, turning to Mindy and Alice.

"Leave mine off most of the time for security purposes," Alice said, her answer sliding out with the burr-free character of a well-practiced lie.

"I never got the hang of the thing," Mindy said before the agent could pursue Alice's pre-fab response. "Might be something wrong with the interface. I don't know, but I can never tell when it's on."

"Have you had it serviced by a professional?" N'onoch inquired.

"Can't afford it."

"Of course not."

N'onoch folded his arms and glared at his subjects. "Your stories have more discrepancies than a loan shark's bank account. But the only crime I might be able to charge you with is taking passage on a vessel without the owner's permission. But even that is problematic. 32's incomplete records, most unfortunately, included his passenger manifest. And he vouches for you having paid after boarding, so I can't prove that you broke any laws.

"If we weren't busy tracking down who was behind the kzinten smuggling, I'd dig deeper into this. But you're small fry and of little interest to the department at this time. So, I'm releasing you. However, I suggest you be extra mindful of galactic laws in the days ahead. If you commit even a minor infraction, I'll reopen this case and haul you back in for deeper interrogation. Mind probes are expensive but effective at gleaning the truth from less cooperative subjects. Am I clear?"

"Yes, sir," Mindy and Alice answered together. Then, before Nick could express his confusion over N'onoch's ability to transmit light through his body, they grabbed the ghoulie by the arms and marched him to the door.

21

On their way out of the interrogation room, Smallberries returned the team's gear. Although the centauran lacked the flexible facial features needed to express emotion, his onyx orbs glittered with unmistakable malice as he returned Nick's backpack.

"You'll make a mistake," he growled. "People like you always do. And when you do, we'll be waiting."

Alice bristled at the threat, but Mindy kept the group moving until they were down the hall and out of hearing.

"Now what?" she asked as they paused at an intersection with a larger corridor.

"We need to go to the maintenance cube, but first we need to visit the morgue," Nick replied.

"Why?"

"It's part of the plan. I'll explain when we get there."

"There's a plan?"

Alice leaned close and whispered in Mindy's ear, something made more than a little terrifying by the slither-click of her razor-sharp mandibles as she spoke.

Mindy's eyes widened as she gave Alice a startled look. "You're kidding! Why didn't you tell—"

"Shh! It'll all come clear shortly."

Nick activated his data link, scanned the wormgate station's corridor map, and said, "Follow me."

Just as they made their way out of the station's security section, a large Thurbian stepped in front of them, blocking their way. Another appeared behind them, blocking any retreat.

"Nick, so glad to see you!" the Thurb chortled, pointing a snub-nosed disrupter pistol at him. "Urk's gonna be thrilled when I tell him I was able to collect your debt."

"But I can't pay yet," Nick said desperately.

"Of course you can. You have something better than credits, and Urk wants it."

"What's that?"

"The coordinates to Altimus. Urk had you tagged with a nano-bug when you returned to the Rigellian, and he heard your plans. And rGov's scanners on this station are so old they never spotted it. Made it easy to track you down after rGov released you. Now give us the earthling, and he'll clear your debt."

Nick looked at Mindy, then back at the goon. "No. I wouldn't trade anybody to Urk for anything."

The Thurb smiled. "Actually, glad you're taking that attitude. I can finish you off and take the earthling anyway."

"Wait! There's no need for violence," Mindy said, taking a step forward. "I'll come quietly. Just let the others go."

Frowning, the thug motioned her forward with his gun. "Pity, I was looking forward to splattering the walls with his guts."

Mindy raised her hands and walked forward. When she reached the Thurb, she suddenly brought her knee up in a classic kick to the groin, a sensitive area shared by a surprisingly large number of the galaxy's bipeds.

"Whuff!" the goon gasped as he folded to the floor, his exclamation cut short by Mindy's knuckle punch to his wind-pipe.

When his partner stepped forward to seize Mindy, Alice casually kicked him in the knee with one of her middle legs.

"Pity rGov took my lucky ring away," she muttered, bending over the prostrate goon and cutting his throat with one quick swipe of her talons. "I hate cleaning Thurb innards off my talons."

Nick stared at the carnage, appalled. "Where did you learn that?" he demanded.

"Missionary work is dangerous," Mindy replied. "So the church gives everybody hand-to-hand combat training after morning mass."

"I think I'm beginning to like this religion of yours," Alice said with a sparkle in her eyes.

Nick blinked and stood silent for a moment. Pulling himself together, he said, "Okay, change of plan. You two go to the maintenance section and hide. I've got something to take care of, then I'll meet you there. Okay?"

"Gotcha," Alice replied with a wink, drawing a confused look from Mindy.

Nick activated his data link and scanned the wormgate station's corridor map. "This facility is of standard configuration. Getting to the maintenance bay will be easy. Alice, take Mindy and follow the directions I just transmitted to you. Wait at the entrance to the maintenance bay until I arrive. Then I'll let us all in."

Alice nodded, then led Mindy off down the corridor.

22

After taking a moment to orient himself, Nick trotted down the hallway in the other direction.

Running, he quickly realized, was a terrible idea, as it required him to take deep breaths of the station's air.

Like all wormhole stations, seventy centuries of continuous operation caused the accumulated smells of all of the varied species that had passed through the station to form a permanent miasma so offensive to olfactory organs that even beings entirely lacking a sense of smell complained about it. In an effort to mitigate the problem, the station purged its atmosphere every ten cycles. Regardless, the stink soon returned, being deeply impregnated in the walls themselves.

"Must be close to their ten-cycle out-gassing," Nick gasped as he paused outside the security area to pull a scarf from his backpack and wrap it around his head, covering his nose and mouth.

Trudging onward, he passed other beings who ignored him completely. The lucky ones wore respirator masks to avoid dealing with the station's aroma; others carried pomanders of fragrant oils in a depressingly vain effort to mask the scent.

Reaching a transport tube, Nick signaled over his comm for a module configured for oxygen breathers from standard gravity. The tube's door opened a moment later to reveal a suitable conveyance pod.

Nick stepped inside and used his personal comm to transmit his desired destination to the pod's control system. There was a brief surge as the unit accelerated away from the security section, followed by occasional bumps and jostlings as it navigated the wormgate's maze of transport tubes until it reached the station's admin module.

Nick slipped out of the pod with a quick look both ways and scampered down the empty corridor. Then, turning left, he went a little further until he reached a doorway labeled "Maintenance Only." He sent a standard access code to the door, and it opened.

Entering, Nick found himself in the maintenance section of the station's morgue, a rarely used area in a section largely avoided by visitors and staff. Whether this was due to the intense cold, a smell that made dead fish hold their nose in disgust, or a general reluctance amongst the population to go near the carcasses of once-sentient beings was moot. The critical thing was that the facility was deserted.

Nick entered the morgue from the maintenance room, a large steel chamber with hundreds of glass-walled bays to hold corpses. There were also a dozen complex tubs in the center of the room, some of which were large enough to hold a whale's body. An automated attendant greeted Nick and promptly gave him the location of Egrog's body.

Nick followed the wall until he reached the specified bay. Then, after a furtive look around to ensure he wasn't being watched, Nick sent a code to the bay to open its door.

Egrog's frost-covered body slid out on a wide metal slab.

"About time!" Egrog sputtered, pouring himself off the slab onto the floor and slowly oozing into his preferred spherical form. "Do you know how cold the morgue is on one of these stations? Brrr! I'm not built for these kinds of temps!"

"I came as soon as rGov let us go," Nick said defensively.

"Okay, no problem. Where are the girls?"

"I sent them to wait at the entrance to the maintenance section."

"Excellent! So, the plan worked."

"So far, it has. Were you able to, er—"

"Smuggle your grav tools aboard? Of course! I mean, that's why we ran this little scam, isn't it? Geez, you shoulda seen the reaction of the agents sent to recover my body. Totally grossed them out, and they were in such a hurry to stuff me in one of the morgue's bays that they didn't bother to scan me for contraband."

Egrog turned a frosty orange and, with a resonant burp, coughed up one of the small aluminum cases holding Nick's grav tools. A few more eructations produced the rest of the ghoulies' gear.

"There you go, bud!" Egrog said, wiping a bit of dribble off a corner of his mouth.

"Thanks!" Nick wiped off his toolset and put it in his backpack. "Are you ready to go?"

"Sure am. Let's get outta this freezer!"

23

The two grifters slipped out of the morgue through the door Nick had used to gain entrance. Then, adopting nonchalant attitudes that drew curious looks from every sentient they passed, they made their way to the nearest transport tube. It took only a few minutes to zip across the station to the maintenance pod, where they found Alice and Mindy waiting.

"Welcome back, lover." Alice glided over to put a possessive arm around the gobbet's torso.

Fuming, Mindy stooped over the gobbet. "You let us think you were dead! Why'd you do that?"

"Sorry," Egrog grinned. "A necessary part of the plan. It was the only way to fool rGov's emotion scanners. They might have detected it if you thought I was still alive."

"But...but Nick and Alice knew!"

"Ghoulies' brains operate in multidimensional space, and conventional scanners can't handle the complexity. And nobody in his right mind wants to know what goes on inside a mantid's skull."

"Hey!" Alice said, her voice going up an octave as she put her arms on her upper hips. "I resent that!"

"Are you saying that humans can't be trusted?"

"No, just that your brain's already been hacked twice, and traces of that might show up even on a superficial scan. It seemed best to be cautious.

"Oh, I get it. No problem."

The expression on Mindy's face made it evident that there was a problem and that it would manifest itself momentarily. Though not the most intuitive individual regarding interspecies conflict, Nick sensed this would be a good time to interrupt the discussion.

"Perhaps this can be discussed later," he said. "Right now, we need to get to the keyhole before rGov realizes what we're doing, or more of Urk's goons track us down."

"Lead on, buddy," Egrog said, his soft rose tint betraying his relief.

Nick led the team into the central bay of the maintenance cube, a chamber twice the size of a football field filled with a tangle of wires, conduits, free-floating circuit boards, and exotic machinery. At the sight of the disordered mess, Mindy exclaimed, "What is all this junk? I thought this was the station's maintenance area?"

"It is," Nick responded.

"But it's a mess! How do you find anything in here?"

"Oh, that's not a problem. The AI units keep track of the location of every part. And most of the gear isn't in here anyway. Devices needing special environmental conditions are kept in separate rooms."

"So, this isn't the whole maintenance area?"

"Nope. The wormgate's maintenance section is a cube a kilometer in size. It contains all the spare parts and instruments needed to keep the station operational. "

"Oh. Well, where's this keyhole Egrog mentioned? And why is it here? What's it for, anyway?"

Nick paused to sort through Mindy's questions before answering.

"There are several keyhole stations in here." Nick gestured toward a nearby corridor. "That leads out of this area and will take you to several of them. Each station generates one of the miniature wormholes that we call keyholes. Maintenance crews use the keyholes to access the station's sealed sections. It's much more efficient to just keyhole into a sealed area than it is to go through the laborious process of unsealing, resealing, and then purging such areas."

"How come they aren't locked down like the big wormhole? Aren't they just as dangerous?"

Nick sighed and stopped to pinch the bridge of his stubby nose, much like a kindergarten teacher about to explain why the sky was blue for the thousandth time.

"Mindy, although keyholes are conceptually identical to full-sized wormholes, they're small, just big enough to pass technicians and their instruments."

"But are they safe?"

"Yes, keyholes are inherently safe. The keyhole stations operate with limited power, which functionally limits how big a keyhole can become. In addition, every part of the system is load-limited to ensure failure if the keyhole gets too big."

"Oh."

Nick led the team down the corridor he'd mentioned to Mindy, stopping in front of a door emblazoned with a warning sign.

"Hey, Nick?"

"Yes, Mindy."

"If these are so handy and safe to use, why don't we have them everywhere?"

Nick pressed his forehead against the door for a few seconds with his eyes closed before answering. "Mindy, keyholes operate outside the central control network that synchronizes passage through wormholes between wormgates. That independent operation is necessary to permit ad hoc access to any area of a station.

"But to answer your question, when a few enterprising criminals used a keyhole to loot the vault of the Xander bank, access to the units was locked down so that only certified grav techs could use them. And just to be clear, having the credentials isn't enough. It takes extensive training and skill to use the system."

"Ah, so that's why Egrog recruited you."

"Yes, Mindy, that and the desire to help a friend out of a jamb. Now please be quiet while I work."

After being released by rGov, Nick found his grav tech credentials restored. Unfortunately, that wasn't enough to access one of the keyhole stations, but he had a solution.

Switching off his comm, he directed his personal comp to access a tiny fiber embedded under his fingernail.

"Hi, Nick!" 32 said. "Looks like our private quantum link is working. How did it go with rGov?"

"They let us go due to insufficient evidence."

32 chuckled. "I told Egrog it would work. Since rGov got hit with budget constraints, they've had to use level five AI units. It wasn't hard for me to outsmart one. Are you at the entrance to the maintenance section now?"

"Yes. Can you convince the security system to let us in?"

"Done. Tricking the local AI was embarrassingly easy. I actually feel sorry for it; it was like taking goomba from a baby wooly-wooly."

"When did you take goomba from a wooly-wooly, and why would you want to do something like that? They just sit down and cry and won't move until you give it back, or they starve to death."

"I didn't actually do that."

"Then why did you say you did?"

32 sighed. "It's just a figure of speech."

"Oh, one of those again."

"Look, can we just get on with the plan?"

Nick scowled. "Sure. But it would be easier if people just said what they mean."

Nick tapped his finger against the doorway. Thanks to 32, he now had full access to the maintenance area and the door opened with a whoosh of stale air.

"Yuck!" Mindy gasped, following him into the room. "I didn't think anything could smell worse than the station air."

"The maintenance area doesn't get purged when the rest of the wormgate does," Nick explained. "That way, the techs can respond to any issues with the purge process without needing environmental suits."

24

Nick led them along a circular hallway until they reached a door marked with warning glyphs identifying it as a keyhole nexus. Once again, the credentials provided by 32 worked to gain entry, and he led the group inside.

The room was round with a slightly domed ceiling. The doorway was the only visible feature in the blank white walls.

Mindy looked around the room. "Where's the control console?"

"Here," Nick answered, tapping his forehead.

"And the keyhole?"

"You're standing inside it. This entire room functions as the nexus for the keyhole. Of course, it can be partitioned into smaller areas. You don't need to move the entire space most of the time."

"So, are you still willing to do this?" she asked. "I know Egrog talked you into it, but it'll be risky on Grunt. As I mentioned, the natives are vicious cannibals. If you don't want to do this, I'll understand."

"I don't have much choice. You saw what Urk's guys were gonna do to me. I need credits, a lot of them, and I need them right away. This looks like my only chance."

Moving quickly to preclude further discussion, Egrog hustled over to Nick and said, "Looks like you've got control of the keyhole. Can you set it up like we discussed?"

"Yep. I've already keyed in the coordinates that Mindy gave us. I can open the keyhole whenever you're ready."

"Wait a sec," Alice said, pushing forward. "We need weapons and survival equipment before we gate to that hellhole."

"And which hellhole would that be?" N'onoch asked from the doorway. "Not planning on an unauthorized trip, are you?"

"What are you doing here, you farking bureaucrat?" Alice demanded.

"Following you. I knew you were up to something when you overrode the transport controls. Now I've caught you, you might as well tell me. I've got enough evidence now to support a warrant for a deep brain scan on each of you, including your 'dead' friend here. I guarantee you won't like that, so you might as well confess now."

Behind his back, Egrog waggled a tentacle at Nick.

Concentrating, Nick opened the keyhole. There was a shimmer as the room was made adjacent to their destination. The result was visually disorienting as their destination image was superimposed on their current location, much like a double-exposed photo.

Nick issued a command to the keyhole controller, and with a push as gentle as a spring breeze, the group passed through the keyhole. The miniature wormhole immediately disappeared, leaving them ankle-deep in fetid muck that extended for several kilometers.

25

"Ew! This stinks worse than the wormgate," Egrog muttered, shuffling back and forth on his feet in a vain effort to minimize contact with slime that smelled like Bombay's sewer but looked far worse, adding hitherto undiscovered hues of yellow and orange to the brown sludge.

"Yeah, welcome to Grunt," Mindy said, pinching her nose shut.

"I thought we were supposed to come through the keyhole near the Temple of Conquest," Alice said, clicking her mandibles in annoyance.

Mindy shaded her eyes with her hand and scanned the surrounding area. "We did. This is only a few hundred meters from where my family's starship landed. As you can see, though, the spaceport is derelict. Nobody's used it in centuries, and the native soil of the planet has covered the concrete."

"This is the native soil of Grunt?"

"Yeah. They don't get rain like Downside, but the soil has such bad drainage that the planet's surface is just one giant swamp."

"How do you know that?"

"We got intensive background info on the trip out. The idea was that we'd stay for a couple of cycles while sharing the gospel with the natives, so we needed to know what we were getting into."

Alice clicked her mandibles in the mantid equivalent of a laugh. "Too bad that didn't include getting into a cookpot."

"Speaking of which, we might want to find a place to hide until we figure out how to approach the Temple without alerting the locals."

"I think it's too late for that," Nick said, backing up until he bumped into Egrog, who was doing the same.

While they'd been talking, a group of natives had silently surrounded them. The grunts were bipedal in form, looking like a cross between a wild boar and a Vogon poet, combining the least appealing aspects of both in one convenient yet unhygienic package. Sporting massive curled tusks and tiny red eyes, they looked just like the cannibals they were reputed to be.

"So nice of you to drop in," one of the grunts said in a voice that would make a gravel crusher cringe. "Early for dinner, though. Where you from? Who are you, and what," he pointed at Egrog, "are you?"

"I…I'm a gobbet," Egrog stammered, multiple eyestalks scanning in all directions in an effort to spot an opening in the grunt ranks. "Name's Egrog."

"I'm Gnash. Are you good to eat?"

"No, we're poisonous. Cause lethal flatulence and make your skin break out in purple warts."

Gnash grinned, hitched up a leg, and loosed an eye-watering blast from his bowels that left a meter-wide dent in the mud behind him. "Worse than that?" Looking down at his arm, which had more in common with the exterior of a rotting fungus than skin, he added, "Purple warts might be an improvement."

"I see. Well, there are many other nasty side effects from consuming raw or cooked gobbet. In fact, there are too many to mention. So if you don't mind, I'll just take my leave and let you go about your business. Sorry to interrupt, whatever it was."

"Our business is to watch the spaceport for unexpected arrivals. Like you."

"Well, you've done a great job of it. Now we'll just be moving along so you can watch for the next group."

"Not so fast!" Gnash grasped Egrog by several legs as the gobbet tried to sidle away. The other grunts leveled Sub-Molecular Arm Cannons at the group.

"Can't you do something, Alice?" Mindy asked desperately.

"Not a chance against those units. You get SMAC'd, you're toast. In your case, probably the whole loaf."

"Silence!" Gnash yelled. "Come with us now, or face our fury!"

"Is it as bad as your flatulence?" Egrog asked, determined to put up a brave front despite being held upside down by his feet.

"Worse," Gnash said with a sneer.

The grunts herded Nick and his friends across the slimy terrain of the spaceport until they reached a large, square building that was either a fragile shade of eggshell or just moldy white, depending on how much purple glurb one had recently ingested.

The inside looked the same as police stations across the galaxy, assuming the locales referenced in the comparison enjoyed the confluence of a vile dictatorship, hereditary corruption, and a universal contempt for hygiene.

"I've seen worse," Egrog muttered as the team was shoved into a holding cell.

"When?" Mindy inquired as she looked around.

"Don't ask," Nick advised, slumping to the floor, then rapidly standing up again. Like what they had waded through outside, muck covered the floor, but it smelled worse and had what appeared to be the remnants of deceased rodent-like creatures floating in it. With no chairs, stools, or furniture in the cell, there was no place to sit or lie down except in the goop. It was a subtle form of torture that portended ill for the group.

"This is your fault!" Alice exclaimed, waving a talon at Egrog. "If you'd had a decent plan, we would have been ready for this. Now we're headed for the cookpot!"

"I have to agree with Alice." Mindy's voice dripped bitterness. "You said you had this covered, but now look at us! I don't want to end up like my parents!"

As the argument escalated, the grunts sauntered off. The team was left alone for several hours, giving them ample time to indulge in every manner of regret, indignation, and blame over their situation.

This merry pastime was interrupted by Gnash pounding an on the cell's iron bars.

"Silence!" he thundered. "Before processing, we need to know how you arrived."

"What kind of processing are you talking about?" Egrog asked, turning dark magenta as he considered the implications.

"Soon enough for that." Gnash chuckled as he pulled up a stool and sat down. "First, how did you get here. Last time we checked, a force field was still blocking access to our planet."

"You still have spacecraft?"

"We build them as we need them."

"When do you need them?"

"When we want to test the force field. If spaceship is vaporized, we shut down production until it's time to try again."

"Oh. Isn't that hard on the crew?"

Gnash shrugged. "You've seen this paradise we call home. The line of volunteers for the test is so long that it takes half a day to walk from the end of the line to the launch pad. But that's neither here nor there."

"It isn't? Well, then where is it?" Nick asked.

There was protracted silence in the prison as every eye swiveled to look at Nick.

Gnash leaned over and nodded sympathetically to Egrog. "I have a cousin like that. Got his head fried in a high-rad field before we could turn off the generator. It must be tough running things with somebody like that on your team."

160

"What do you mean by that?" Nick demanded, stepping close to the bars.

"Nothing," Mindy said, taking Nick by his shoulders and pulling him back.

"But he made no sense!"

"It's just one of those sayings. Just let it go."

"Well, I wish people would be clearer," Nick muttered.

"What's clear," Gnash said with a knowing smile, "is that you have arrived without a spaceship. I don't see any overnight bags, so you weren't planning to stay long. You must have a plan for getting off-planet. A wormhole, perhaps?" He leaned forward. "Something we are very interested in. Tell me how you planned to leave."

"And if we don't?" Egrog asked, regretting the words as soon as they slipped out of his mouth.

"Then one of you will be a featured guest for dinner tomorrow evening. I'll leave you to think about that while you enjoy your accommodations for the night. Perhaps one of you will share your secret with me tomorrow morning."

26

After Gnash left, the group huddled together.

"We need to get out of here before daybreak, or we'll all end up in the stew pot," Egrog said.

"But how?" Nick asked. "We're locked in an iron cage, and three armed guards are in the room outside. Even if we got through the bars, they'd recapture us immediately."

Alice stamped her foot in frustration, splashing gook on the walls. "If I had any of my farking weapons that rGov took away, we could shoot our way out. Or slash; if I had something sharp and hard enough to cut steel, I could make that work."

"That might not be necessary," Mindy said.

"How so?"

"Wait till dark," she replied, then went to stand in the corner of the cell with her arms folded over her breasts.

Egrog tried to cajole more information from her, but she remained silent.

There was no light in the cell, and when night fell, it was so dark even Alice had trouble seeing.

"This will do," Mindy said as she crouched by the bars at the front of the cell and let one of her arms drop to her side. Then, bending her head down, she made little wheedling and whistling noises until a tiny, furry head popped up between her breasts.

"Dinner time, Bumpkiss," she whispered.

Nick backed up against a cell wall and then stood still. Alice made it to the ceiling in one bound and hung there in a defensive posture. Egrog flattened himself against the cell's back wall. Three weeks of close contact in the cargo ship hadn't lessened the team's instinctive fear of the kzinten.

Bumpkiss hopped out of his hiding spot and landed in the muck.

He made plaintive *meep, meep* noises as he tried to shake the sludge off his tiny paws. The sounds were loud enough to draw the attention of one of the guards, who sauntered over, SMAC gun dangling from one hand.

"Kzinten!" the guard screamed when he saw what was making the noise.

"Hic, hic!" Bumpkiss cried as he launched himself between the bars.

The grunt's body landed with a wet plop on the floor, but the sound, like his scream, came too late to warn the other guards. Bumpkiss had ripped the throats out of all three before the first hit the ground.

"Nice job," Egrog said, sidling up to the bars furthest from Bumpkiss. "Now it's my turn."

Flattening his bulk, Egrog slid effortlessly between the bars and, in a moment, was standing in front of the cell's door.

"Never met a lock I couldn't pick." Egrog oozed confidence as he wormed his tendrils behind the face plate of the door lock's keypad. Seconds later, a loud sizzling noise accompanied by a shower of sparks sent Egrog flying across the room.

"Are you okay?" Nick asked, watching his friend twitch in the muck.

"I'm fine." His skin dark purple with embarrassment, Egrog pulled himself back into his preferred spheroid shape and stood up on a dozen shaky legs. "But this is gonna be a problem."

"!#Perhaps not," 32 said to Nick on his embedded quantum link.

"Why not? We're still locked in."

"True, but not for long. I was following your exploits over the visual channel of our quantum link and observed the guard's actions as he keyed in the lock code."

"So? He was on the other side of the door, and I couldn't see what he typed."

"Yes, but the motions of his arm were clear. Using your friend's size for comparison, I could compute the dimensions of the keypad, confirming my hypothesis that the grunts just cloned a type 43 design, which is common throughout the galaxy."

"Brilliant. How does that help us get out of jail?"

"With the unit's dimensions and the relative motions of the guard's arm, I could deduce the pass code he entered."

After a long pause, Nick asked, *"well, what was it?"*

"Oh, yes, well, it goes like this: 'Wooga booga karth mucklu snargle prat,' which translates to 'Gnash is a jerk' in grunt."

"Please spell that slowly, so I can tell Egrog what to enter."

It took a minute before Nick could convince Egrog to approach the door's keypad again, but after the gobbet entered the code, the door opened with a squeal of offended metal.

Alice was first out, dropping from the ceiling to grab a SMAC gun from one of the defunct guards. "Let's get outta here," she called as she made for the exit.

"Wait," Mindy said. "Bumpkiss is still eating."

Nick's stomach churned as he watched the kzinten gnaw its way into one of the guard's chests to get to the organ meat.

"But we need to escape while we have a chance!"

Egrog held up a cautionary tendril. "Do you really want to interrupt a kzinten in the middle of its meal?"

Alice looked back. Bumpkiss looked up at her, blood dripping from his tiny maw.

"Now that you mention it, I wouldn't want to rush the little fellow. Let's let him finish."

"Wise choice. While we're waiting, Mindy, do you think you could find the Temple of Conquest from here? Or do we need to convince one of the local boys to tell us?"

"I think I can. The Temple was a half-days walk south from the coordinates where we came through the keyhole. I'm pretty sure the guards marched us due east for about three hours. So if we head south-west from here, we should reach the Temple in about five hours.

"That'll put us there around daybreak if we leave now."

Everybody looked at Bumpkiss, who proved to be a good eater for such a little fellow.

Half the guard's internal organs had disappeared, though the kzinten did not appear appreciably larger for devouring such a bulk of protein. Where the creature put the mass would have made an intriguing topic of research in multi-dimensional storage topography, yielding startling insights about the ability of organic beings to perform energy/mass transport over quantum tunnels in real-time, but unfortunately for galactic science, the only people present were fixated on the kzinten's chilling ability to chew through bone as easily as fat.

After a few tense minutes, Bumpkiss finished his feast. He let out a dainty burp, licked himself clean, and then perched on the guard's head, making bouncing motions toward Mindy.

"All done? Good boy!" Mindy opened her arms to receive the kzinten as it leaped to her breast. It disappeared into her substantial cleavage, and, one arm folded under her breasts, she nodded for Egrog to leave.

Alice led the way out, leaping through the jail's entrance with a SMAC gun in each hand. Pouting with disappointment at finding no ready targets, she lowered the guns and motioned for the others to follow.

Egrog flattened out his feet until they looked like the appendages of waterfowl in popular children's animations and could waddle across the muck's surface without sinking in. The rest of the team struggled to keep up, their feet sinking ankle-deep in the pervasive mud.

27

The few buildings in the vicinity of the jail were industrial in nature and had been abandoned ages ago when the spaceport was closed. With the guards down, there were no other grunts in the area, and the team escaped without notice despite their slow, noisy progress.

What they failed to take into account was that their footprints remained in the muck long after they were gone, leaving a trail that even Gnash's mentally challenged cousin could follow.

Throughout the night, they trudged onwards. Nick found it harder to lift his legs with each step as the glop sucked at his feet, pulling them down with unrelenting sadism.

Sunrise found them close to their destination and even closer to physical collapse.

"I think that's it," Mindy gasped, pointing to a large structure in the center of a group of abandoned buildings.

"Super! At this pace, we should be there in—" Egrog paused as a siren sounded behind them, followed by the crackle of SMAC guns and the chime of harmonic disrupters. "That doesn't sound good. Maybe we should pick up the pace."

Aching legs pumping through the muck, the group ran as best they could toward the Temple.

When they reached the entrance, they paused to catch their breath.

At that moment, an intense flash of violet light reflected off the nearby buildings, followed ten seconds later by the deafening silence of an implosion bomb. Based on a miniature black hole, the weapon swallowed everything within a hundred-meter radius, including the sound of its own detonation, which nonetheless still hurt the ears.

"Everybody down!" Alice screamed, and they dove face-first into the slime. The wave of displaced air racing to fill the void created by the implosion tumbled them across the ground for several seconds before relenting.

Looking back, Alice said, "Aircars! Coming this way!"

"Into the building, quick!" Egrog yelled.

Following the gobbet, the team staggered through the doors and then paused.

As vile and frankly gauche as the surface of Grunt was, the Temple was equally serene and elegant. Ivory columns supported a green marble dome that arched high above their heads. The floor was paved with large squares of pink granite flecked with gold, and the restrained umber of the walls was accented with white niches containing objects of incredible beauty. Objects that the grunts had pilfered from scores of worlds before rGov stopped their rampage.

"The grunts built this?" Nick said in disbelief.

Egrog looked around and shook his head. "No, I don't think so. According to some of the legends, they made their conquered subjects build it for them."

Alice clicked her talons in annoyance. "That's nice to know, but shouldn't we be looking for the Altimus exhibit instead of discussing aesthetics, lover boy? I'd like to find it before the filthy grunts or whoever they just tangled with catch up with us. Mindy, do you remember where the exhibit was?"

"No, it's been too long since I was here to remember any details. It was in one of the side halls toward the back of the Temple, but I can't recall which one."

"Then we'll have to search for it."

"It will go faster if we split up," Egrog said.

"Great idea! I'm with you, sweetie-pie. You have no idea how I mourned your demise. Once we're alone, we can make up for lost time."

"Uh, yeah, but I'd rather, ahem, well, I think we need to think ahead."

"Ooo, kinky!"

"No! What I meant was, I think you should go with Nicky."

"Me?" Nick squeaked.

"Yes. Definitely. We can't get back to the wormgate or go on to Altimus without you, so you need protection in this hostile environment. Alice can do that better than any of us."

Alice stamped a foot in annoyance. "Why not Mindy? She's got the pox-cursed kzinten trained, and it's positively lethal."

"Do you really want to turn that thing loose?"

Alice paused, her protruding eyes turning to look at each other as she contemplated that thought. "Nick, you're with me. Let's move!" Turning to face the back of the Temple, she grabbed Nick by his shirt sleeve and dragged him away.

28

From the magnificent, domed entrance, a vaulted corridor extended to the back of the Temple with hallways branching off from it at regular intervals.

Nick and Alice started at the furthest hall on the right side of the Temple and began working their way back toward the front. As Mindy had promised, each exhibit had a star map, a 3D hologram of the conquered world, and an array of artifacts from that world. There seemed to be an emphasis on bright shiny objects, and Nick wondered if that was a reflection of the intellectual development of the grunts. Interspersed amongst the looted items were images of destroyed cities and smoking battlefields, arranged so that the beauty of the objects contrasted subtly with the horrific scenes in the holograms, creating a state of cognitive dissonance. The effect was so far beyond the stunted esthetics of the grunts that it almost certainly was a seditious statement by the artisans forced to create the exhibits.

Whenever Nick lingered to examine a particularly bewitching vase or statuette, Alice pulled him away.

"We don't have time for sight-seeing, short stuff. Let's get this job done and get out of this Hive-mother-cursed temple!"

Nick and Alice were just finishing the examination of an exhibit on the second floor when they heard shouting.

"Hold on," Alice growled, scooping Nick up with a middle leg as she scampered up the wall onto the ceiling. Taking advantage of the deep shadows caused by the dark wooden beams crisscrossing the marble, she skulked across unseen, stopping directly above three Dweebians holding Mindy captive.

Shinnying down the chain supporting one of the pendant lights, she screamed, "Freeze!" as she brandished one of the SMAC guns in her free hand and opened her mandibles in a terrifying display of dentition that would make a surgeon's scalpel look dull.

The two thugs holding Mindy dropped their disrupter pistols and let her go, raising their hands. The third thug took a millisecond to wet his pants before doing likewise. The sight of a mantid in full-on berserker mode generally caused the galaxy's better-informed citizens to scan for the closest exit while simultaneously wondering if they had filed the latest copy of their will with rGov.

Hanging upside down from Alice's leg, Nick had just enough time to feel relief that they had successfully rescued Mindy when the delicate marble beam to which the pendant's chain was attached collapsed from their combined weight. Alice face-planted on the granite floor, and Nick landed on the stunned mantid's head. With a violent twitch, she rolled onto her back, legs curled up like a stunned spider, a comparison that would have annoyed her if she were conscious, given the enduring animosity between sentient insects and arachnids.

Pulling the SMAC gun from her limp fingers, the Dweebian in charge chortled and kicked her thorax several times. "Not so tough now, eh?"

"Stop that!" Mindy yelled, kicking at the Dweebian's shins.

"You're in no position to shoot your mouth off," the thug replied, slapping her hard enough to knock her down.

Nick wondered why she hadn't unleashed the kzinten when he noticed that her torso was wrapped in a fine net of translucent titanium that even a kzinten couldn't chew through. He struggled to his feet and stepped between the Dweebian and Mindy.

"What do you think you're doing, little fella?" the thug chuckled, looking down at the ghoulie, who barely reached his belt buckle.

"This," Nick replied, rabbit-punching the Dweebian in the family jewels.

Although the technique was effective, it only put one of Urk's goons out of commission. The other two pounced on Nick and quickly restrained him in the same mesh wrapped around Mindy. They trussed up Alice similarly, then one used a chin mike to report their status. Within a few minutes, Urk himself appeared, accompanied by half a dozen henchmen.

A renegade centauran, Urk combined the brilliant mind and single-minded pursuit of goals characteristic of his species with a profoundly broken moral compass and a complete disregard for the restraints of civilization. The one time when rGov had managed to bring him into custody, the psycho-technicians had had such difficulty evaluating him with the standard checklist for sociopathic behavior that they revised the checklist to include over a dozen new entries.

"Well, well," he said, rubbing his hands together with satisfaction as he examined the net holding Alice. "Looks like the spider got caught in a web instead of her victims. Heh! And my favorite ghoulie, too. Hey Nicky, got my credits? No? Didn't think so. Heh, you'll pay one way or another, and after the trouble you've caused me, I'm looking forward to 'other.'"

Urk looked at Mindy, who had managed to hitch herself up into a sitting position with her back against a wall.

"And you must be the earthling our late gobbet friend was working with. So sad to read about his demise from kzinten poisoning on the wormgate's news feed. Heh! I do appreciate your leading me here. Finding Altimus is going to set me up for life. I'll be so rich rGov won't dare touch me. But that doesn't offset the trouble you've caused me by interfering with my shipment of kzintens. I lost a lot of credits on that deal, and you'll pay for that.

"By the way, how's that symbiotic thing going with the kzinten you've got trapped against your chest? What do you suppose will happen when it gets hungry but can't get out of the mesh to feed? Hmmm, should be fun to watch."

"You won't get away with this," Mindy said with a glare.

"Of course I will. Who's going to stop me?"

"rGov will if the grunts don't get you first. And I hope they do. I'd like to see your skinny centauran ass dunked in a cauldron of boiling oil."

"If you're talking about your erstwhile captor, Gnash, I'm afraid he's not going to be joining us or anybody else for dinner tonight or any other night. Every grunt that knew we were here was vaporized a half hour ago."

"Oh yeah? Then how'd you find us if Gnash didn't tell you?"

"Easy. We just followed your tracks in the mud. It must have been quite a trudge for you. Your footsteps were ankle-deep the whole way."

"Oh. Well, how'd you even know we were here?"

"Equally easy. The tracker on Nick led us to the keyhole generator on the wormgate station before he disappeared from our scanners. All we had to do was hack the keyhole's control system to find the last planetary address entered." Urk looked at Nick. "By the way, that was a clever trick, putting the controller into a loop so it would dial back for ten minutes every day, giving yourself a chance to escape this cesspool planet. Without a grav tech, I wouldn't have been able to operate the system. But the auto dial-back made it easy for me to follow you here, and it's going to make it easy for me to get away. Heh."

Urk turned to his minions and gestured down the hall. "Split up, and search for the Altimus exhibit. Ping me when you find it."

The motley crew of Dweebian and Thurbian gangsters scattered, leaving only two with Urk to watch the captives.

"This might take a while," Urk said, correctly estimating the abilities of his associates as he squatted next to Nick. "Which gives me plenty of time to collect on your debt." Tilting his head to the side, he reached out and tweaked one of Nick's antenna horns with a fingertip, chuckling as Nick twitched in distress.

"Pretty sensitive area, isn't it? I understand that a ghoulie has a greater concentration of nerve endings in its antenna than can be found in any other sentient being. Heh. Really opens up the options for inflicting pain, eh? What should I use first? Heat? Cold? Pressure?" Urk sat back on his heels and stroked his chin with a thoughtful smile that made Nick's stomach churn.

A call came in before Urk could start, and he stood up. "Looks like the fun will have to wait a bit," he said, clearly disappointed. "One of my boys has already found the Altimus exhibit.

"Watch these folk till I get back," he told the Dweebians who had remained with him. Then he strolled away, eventually disappearing into the gloom of a side-hall near the end of the Temple.

Nick watched the Dweebians with interest as they stood beside each other, showing off their tattoos. Unfortunately for them, they were oblivious to a pair of sledgehammers slowly descending from the ceiling on a pair of red tentacles. Nick winced in anticipation as the hammers swung back, causing the Dweebians to turn and stare at him in perplexity. As a result, they never saw what hit them, dropping to the ground like oodlebugs flying into an electric grid.

"Thanks, Egrog!" Nick grinned as his friend oozed down from the ceiling, reforming into his preferred globular form upon reaching the ground.

"Not so loud. Urk will be back shortly, and we need to clear out before he shows."

"Shows what?"

"Never mind, we just need to leave and leave fast."

Egrog struggled for a minute but couldn't find a latch or release mechanism for the nets holding his team captive. "Dang, there must be a way to get these off!"

"There is, but you need the right tool to do it."

"What?" Egrog jumped in surprise as Urk appeared from the shadows along with half a dozen of his gang.

"Did you really think I'd fall for a trick like that?" Urk said, leveling a disrupter pistol at Egrog's center of mass.

"Like what?"

"Like finding the Altimus exhibit in less than a minute after beginning the search. I figured it was staged to draw me away from my victims, so I played along. Once out of sight, I doubled back with my associates to see what or who showed up. Now that I've got all of you, I can take my time looting this place. Heh! Even if we don't find the map to Altimus, there's enough treasure here to put me in the pink for cycles."

"Is it good to be in the pink?" Nick whispered to Mindy.

Before she could reply, he heard the sinister sound of the safeties being released on dozens of hand weapons from shadows even deeper and darker than the deep dark shadows that had hidden Urk.

"Unlikely that he'll find out," N'onoch said, stepping into the light.

29

Pointing a small laser gun at Urk, N'onoch said, "Detective Smallberries, take Urk and his gang into custody, then release their captives."

"You won't take me that easy," Urk said, leveling his pistol at the rGov agent.

As he did, a dozen deputies and a half-dozen stubby combat bots stepped forward to support N'onoch. Dressed in red, combat-grade body armor and carrying infinite-cycle harmonic disrupters, the deputies provided a sufficiently convincing counter-argument that Urk's people dropped their weapons and surrendered without hesitation.

Tossing down his gun in disgust, Urk said, "Fine, you got the drop on me. But this would've played out differently if I wasn't surrounded by a bunch of liverless cowards. Just remember, taking me and taking me in are two different things. This ain't over."

"Oh, it's over," Smallberries growled as he slipped a restraint collar around Urk's neck. The other criminals were similarly restrained, and then Nick and his friends were released from their nets. Smallberries took Urk by the shirt front and said, "I'm personally escorting you to your cell."

"Not so fast," Gnash snarled, stepping out of a hidden doorway with a platoon of heavily armed and seriously annoyed grunt infantry. "These characters flattened a guard shack and a squad of my men. The only cell they're visiting is the one next to the community cook pot."

N'onoch folded his arms as he faced the grunt commander. "I respect your position, but I have to reject your request. I'm not turning over our prisoners, not even a sadistic criminal like Urk, to you so they can be fricasseed and served for dinner."

Gnash grinned, revealing a magnificent array of dentation that would make a shark envious. "It wasn't a request. We got more guns than you and a lot less to lose."

"Really? I have an armored patrol craft sitting outside the front door and a planetary assault destroyer ten klicks overhead that say otherwise. Not to mention the drone swarm next to the ceiling that you have overlooked. No, we're taking these individuals with us and leaving now."

Gnash ground his teeth together, giving Nick sudden insight into how he got his name. "Like I said, we've got nothing to lose."

As the standoff between Gnash and N'onoch escalated, Nick noticed a sly grin on Urk's face. Fascinated, he watched a thin black line appear out of the corner of Urk's mouth, resolving into a hair-thin worm. It slid down Urk's cheek to where the restraining collar was fastened, then coiled around the collar.

With sudden insight, Nick realized that the worm must be a symbiont that Urk carried just for this purpose. Restraining collars attached to a perp's nervous system prevented them from specific actions, including removing the collar. But the collar only worked on the being to which it was attached, and a symbiont would be unaffected. The collar separated and fell from Urk's neck without a sound, and he caught it as it fell to prevent it from banging off the floor.

Reaching into his ear, Urk extracted a tiny yellow bead that could easily be mistaken for ear wax, but Nick was confident that it was something more sinister. A moment later, he was proven right as Urk tossed the bead to the ground between Gnash and N'onoch. It exploded with a blinding flash and filled the area with dense yellow smoke.

Urk ducked through one of the hidden doors the grunts had used to enter the chamber, disappearing just as the first shots whickered through the saffron gloom.

"Get down!" Egrog yelled, pulling Mindy to the floor. Nick pancaked next to Alice, who was still lying on her back, imitating a defunct spider.

"We've got to get out of here!" Mindy cried.

"Follow Urk. He must know a way out!"

Nick took one of Alice's arms while Mindy and Egrog grabbed the rest of her appendages and, with a desperate heave, pulled her body through the same opening Urk had used.

Egrog sent eyeball tentacles in all directions, then extruded a hand and slapped a large round button by the door. The door pivoted shut with a sound like a stone boat dragged across gravel, leaving the group in the dark.

"I can't see a thing," Mindy said. "Has anybody got a light?"

"Not me," Egrog and Nick replied.

The group sat in the dark for a few moments, growing increasingly frightened as the sounds of conflict from the other side of the door escalated.

"We should try to get out of here," Egrog said.

"Sure. Which way do you want to go?" Mindy replied sarcastically.

"Does it matter? Just help me with Alice and—"

"Unnh," Alice groaned, then suddenly screamed, "Incoming! Hit the dirt! Hit the dirt!"

"What good will it do to strike the ground," Nick asked, only to be shushed by the rest of the team.

"Ah, Alice, are you okay?" Egrog ventured.

"Oh, yeah. My noggin feels like somebody dropped a rock on it, though."

"That was probably me," Nick said.

"Can you stand?" Egrog asked.

"Yeah. Give me a sec…okay, yeah, I'm a bit wobbly, but I've seen worse. Why are we sitting in a darkened room? And what's happening on the other side of this wall? Sounds like somebody's having fun."

"That's Gnash and N'onoch's men shooting it out. We dove in here for cover."

"And your next step?"

"Don't know. Can't see in the dark, so we don't know which way to go."

"Why don't you turn on the light?"

"What light?"

There was a click as Alice flicked a light switch next to the door, and the room filled with soft green light. They were in a wide hallway made of smooth gray stone.

"You didn't see the farking switch?" Alice asked.

"I couldn't see my own eye stalks! Thanks!"

30

Egrog looked around, then pointed to a flight of stairs at the end of the corridor. "Let's head down there. It's only a matter of time before one of those boys out there lights off some heavy ordinance, and it'll be much safer below ground level."

The group scampered to the stairwell, but as they started down, Alice lagged behind. The stairway made several turns, carrying them well below ground before Alice suddenly said, "Stop!"

"What? What's wrong?!" Egrog asked.

"There's something wrong here."

"What?"

"Look at the walls."

"They're gray. So?"

"And clean. So's the floor."

"Well, the Temple's well kept-up. What's the problem."

"That. Precisely that. What do we know about the grunts?"

"They're cannibals with stunted aesthetic sensibilities and no sense of humor?"

"They're wattle-assed slobs. I doubt there's a mop or broom on the entire planet. But this place is spotless. Why?"

Egrog looked around, something made easy by his ability to extrude a dozen eyestalks and look in every direction at once.

"Now that you mention it, it is weird. Do you suppose they have robo-janitors like other civilized worlds?"

"If they did, they'd use them to clean up the mess topside. No, there's somebody else here. Somebody that understands fundamental concepts of sanitation and cleanliness. We're not alone."

"I don't see anybody. Or hear anything."

Alice turned to go back up the stairs. "I feel naked without a gun. We need to go back and see if we can liberate some weapons. The way they're slinging ordinance around, there's bound to be casualties we can loot. I'm no fan of rGov agents, but I've developed a real dislike for those grunt bastards. This seems like a good chance to get even with the wibble-faced dirtbags."

"No," Egrog said, putting several restraining hands on Alice's arm. "It's too dangerous, just let it go. It's not your circus and not your monkey. We need to get out of here while we're still taking oxygen through the factory tubing, if you know what I mean?"

Alice scowled. "Fine. But keep those peepers open. And let's move quietly. I'd hate to be surprised by somebody more evolved than the grunts."

"That includes most of the sentient and near-sentient beings in the universe," Mindy quipped.

"What's that about a circus?" Nick whispered to Egrog.

"Just an earthling expression."

"Oh. And the monkey?"

Egrog stopped. "Nick?"

"Yes?"

"Be quiet."

"No way to treat your friends," Nick muttered as he fell in behind Mindy.

After going down several more flights, the stairs opened into an ill-lit corridor that stretched out of sight. Doors appeared at regular intervals along the hallway, and the first dozen that the group passed were closed.

When they reached an open doorway, Mindy held up a hand to stop everybody while she crept forward. After a moment, she motioned the group to follow her in.

A half-dozen beings huddled in the corner of a large room. The only furniture was a long, plain table and several chairs, which the people had piled in front of them in a pathetic effort at a defensive barrier.

As he advanced into the room, Nick saw two centauran, a couple of Dweebians, a Thurb, and a Dimwittle.

"It's okay, we're not going to hurt you," Egrog said, the fear-induced magenta tint of this body at odds with his smooth, con-man tone of voice.

One of the centaurans inched forward. "Are you—did they—how did you get here?"

"We're just passing through. Don't suppose you could show us the way out of the Temple?"

"Leaving is easy. But nobody who goes outside comes back."

"Why not?"

"The grunts…"

"Oh, yeah. So you've been trapped down here for how long?"

"I'm F'stick. I was chief steward of a star-liner until about a decade ago. When the wormhole generator on our ship malfunctioned, we emerged on the wrong side of Grunt's force field and crashed. The grunts swarmed us as our emergency shuttles landed. rGov pulled most of the survivors out, but we got separated from the rest. We hid in the Temple for a few days but soon realized we'd been written off for dead."

"How did you stay alive so long?"

The centauran looked down, clearly ashamed. "We made a deal with the grunts. They leave us alone as long as we keep the Temple clean and in good repair. Mostly. But once a cycle, we draw straws. There used to be a lot more of us."

"I see. Well, this is your lucky day. rGov has a patrol ship parked outside the main entrance with enough troops to put a serious crimp in the grunt's dinner plans. Show us how to get out of here, and we'll help you get to the ship."

"How do we know it's not a trap?"

"Would I lie to you?"

F'stick sniffed. "I've seen your kind before, gobbet, and there's not an honest bone in your body. What's your angle?"

Egrog shifted nervously, and Nick stared at him with sudden suspicion. "You found it, didn't you?"

"Yeah."

"Why didn't you say so?"

"It's not that simple."

"It's not?"

Mindy huffed in annoyance. "No, it's not. Egrog got distracted with the other loot, and Urk's goons caught us before we could get the coordinates off the display."

"So all this was for nothing?"

"It doesn't have to be," Egrog said, purpling with frustration. "If these good folk would just lead us to the Altimus exhibit on the way out, everybody wins."

F'stick folded his arms. "So that's your scheme. The Altimus exhibit is at the rear of the Temple, but the rGov ship is at the front entrance. Were you planning to ditch us as soon as you got what you wanted?"

"Uh, nothing like that," Egrog stammered, pink with embarrassment. "I would let the agents know you were here, then stand back to let them do their job. They're much better at this rescue business than we are."

"Egrog," Nick said, "We have to help these folk."

"Sure, Nicky."

"No, I mean it, Egrog. Promise on your birth stone."

Egrog went dark purple with embarrassment. "How dare you mention that? That's a private thing, like your antennae. I should never have shared it with you."

"Probably. But it's the only thing you hold sacred enough that you'll keep your word."

"This is dirty pool, Nicky."

Nick looked around. "I don't see any pool, and the place looks clean. Quit stalling, and give me your word you'll help these folk." He could feel eyes on his back, and he shuffled back and forth on his feet, waiting for Egrog to answer.

"Fine, but I'm blaming you if we all get killed."

"Uh, there's one other thing," F'stick said hesitantly.

"Oh gee, you want a cut of the take, don't you?"

"No. But, well, we're not the only beings down here."

"There are other refugees from the grunts?"

"Not exactly. In fact, kind of the opposite."

"I don't follow."

"Have you ever heard of a jabber from Wochness?"

In his travels, Nick had observed that there are two varieties of cursing prevalent in the galaxy: the milder version comprises expletives that are vulgar or offensive to a genteel sentient, whereas the industrial-strength version requires either the invocation of one or more deities with the express intent of consigning the object of imprecation to an over-heated subterranean domain, or the suggestion that a being's immediate ancestry is sufficiently ill-defined as to preclude any rigorous genealogical study.

Alice was a master of both.

Nick watched in awe as she dropped the chair she'd been breaking apart for a club and gave vent to a torrent of such vivid curses that Mindy covered her ears, Egrog purpled with embarrassment, and Nick felt his antennae shrinking in their protective horns. When finished, she sat down and refused to speak, idly thumping her makeshift club on the floor.

Puzzled, Egrog finally asked F'stick, "What is it?"

"Sentient carnivore, looks like a twenty-meter-long snake with wings. Its eyes glow like lava, and it's covered in black scales. Has a taste for raw brains and bad poetry."

Nick and Egrog exchanged looks.

"Why haven't the grunts killed and eaten it?" Nick asked.

"Those black scales are resistant to every weapon in the grunt's arsenal. Whenever the grunts come up with something new, they bring it down here to test. Sometimes the screams last quite a while. I think it likes to play with its food for a bit before getting down to business."

"Oh."

Egrog thought for several minutes before asking, "Do you know where it has its lair? Maybe we can just sneak by."

"It usually lurks in the hallway you just came through. I guess the commotion above got its interest, and it's watching the battle from a higher vantage point."

Egrog scratched the top of his body in thought for a minute, then said, "That could work for us. You said the Altimus exhibit is at the other end of the building. So if the jabber is busy watching the fight near the entrance, we should clearly go in the other direction. Then, after getting the coordinates, we can slip out a side door and make our getaway."

"And what about us?" F'stick asked. "Are you just going to abandon us once you get out?"

"No, no, no. I meant to say that we can show you where the rGov boat is as soon as we get out, and then you can make your way to safety."

"Sounds a lot like you'll abandon us."

"No, I promise. Now let's get going while the jabber is still distracted."

After coaxing Alice out of her uncharacteristic funk, Egrog followed F'stick out the door, turning left down the hallway toward the back of the Temple. At Egrog's insistence, everybody took a chair leg to use as a club on the blatantly fallacious idea that they could be used to defend themselves from a creature that was immune to a harmonic disrupter.

31

After going a few hundred meters, F'stick led the group down a hall that branched off to the right from the main corridor. Several of the lights in the ceiling were out, and as F'stick led them through a maze of corridors, the level of repair declined so that soon they were traveling in near-darkness. As they progressed, it became clear that the underground corridors extended well past the Temple itself, possibly underpinning the entire complex of the abandoned spaceport, which extended for over a dozen kilometers. The ventilation system had clearly malfunctioned, and the air was hot and stale.

Egrog and his team stayed close behind F'stick and didn't notice as the rest of the centauran's group began to fall behind.

"Kinda stuffy in here," Egrog muttered. "And what's that smell?"

"Nothing to worry about," F'stick said casually. "This end of the Temple hasn't seen the same level of maintenance as the rest of the building."

"Why's that?"

F'stick suddenly ducked into a side room. As he slammed the door shut, he said, "Because this is the jabber's favorite hunting ground."

"What?!" Egrog stopped to look around, discovering that he and his team were alone in the gloom.

"This can't be good," Mindy ventured, sidling closer to Alice.

"I wish I was back on the front lines," Alice said emphatically. "A nice clean death. Vaporized in a moment of glory. Not having my farking brains chewed on by a soul-sucking monster!"

"Who's a soul-sucking monster?" the jabber said in a voice like black iron dragged over a tombstone as it swept out of a hidden alcove.

"Run!" screamed Egrog. Extruding a dozen extra feet, he bolted back down the corridor with the rest of the team close behind.

They took several turns down blind corridors until they reached a dead end. Alice forced open a door, but Mindy stumbled and fell as they pushed into the room.

"We've got to help her!" Nick cried.

"Close the door and save yourselves!" Mindy yelled, but Nick wedged into the doorway, reaching out to her with a free hand.

"Take my hand, hurry!" he called.

"It's too late! The jabber's here!"

As Mindy spoke, twenty meters of black death slithered into the hallway, its red eyes fixed on her supine form.

Nick closed his eyes, unable to watch what was about to happen, but he opened them in surprise when he heard, "*hic, hic, hic.*" The kzinten Bumpkiss had bravely taken a defensive position between the jabber and Mindy.

Nobody was more surprised than the jabber, who stopped and stared at the creature for several moments before saying,

> "What tiny thing doth stand before,
>
> this unmatched carnivore?
>
> Are my limbs withered, frail and old,
>
> that one so small should be so bold?"

"Hic, hic, hic!"

The jabber's head reared up, and it scratched its chin with a taloned claw sending a shower of sparks across the hallway.

> "Not for eons have I heard that tongue.
>
> now memory must a long course run
>
> recall from a past long forgotten
>
> to make sense of what has just been spoken."

The jabber bent down until its head was on a level with Bumpkiss.

> "How did you come here? Where have you been?
>
> long have your kind been lost to our ken,
>
> who once rode the skies above Alphanor

on Wochness, hunting direbeasts across the moor?

Bumpkiss tilted his head to the side and bounced on his front paws like a puppy welcoming his master home at the end of a long day.

"Hic! Hic, hic!"

Mindy sat up, eyes blinking in bewilderment, pleasantly surprised that she hadn't yet been dismembered.

"Do you, do you know each other?"

The jabber looked up at her.

"Battle-brothers of old are we."

"But 32 said that the kzinten are from Darkspore in the Orion Nebula near the outer rim, and F'stick said you're from Wochness, near the galactic center."

The jabber laid its head on the floor next to Bumpkiss, who began stropping it like a friendly cat. Then, after a deep sigh, it said, "That is a tale too long and sad to tell properly, which would be in heroic couplets. Unfortunately, your kind are so short-lived that you would pass away before I finished the introduction. So I'll give you a condensed and linguistically uninteresting version."

"My name is Silverblade, and I hatched on the planet Wochness thirty eons before your galactic federation was formed.

"Wochness' gravity was a third of this blighted world's, and I spent long cycles flying its topaz skies in the company of my brothers as we fought the fell armies of the dark horde who sought to conquer our world. The kzinten rode upon our backs in crystal-blue armor, wielding spears of vermillion light. Together, we struck like lightening falling from the sky, and our foes trembled and fled before us.

"But the night-mages of the horde knew a science beyond our own, and when they saw that their defeat was inevitable, they chose to destroy the world before yielding it to their enemies.

"A few of us managed to escape the cataclysm as our sun went nova, but our ships were scattered by the blast, and the one I rode carried none of our battle brothers.

"We searched through the eons but were few and the stars endless. Never did we find any others of our kind or of the kzinten. I lost touch with the last of my people two thousand cycles ago when my scout ship crashed upon this world. I have been trapped here ever since."

"That's an amazing story," Mindy said.

"Is it true?" Egrog asked, poking an eyestalk through the doorway.

Silverblade glared at the gobbet, and Egrog hastily withdrew back into the room.

"I may be getting a bit on in age, but my memory is still good after sixty-odd thousand cycles. And the kzinten will vouch for me if you ask it."

"But they can't speak!" Nick said. "32 said they're sub-sentient." Immediately regretting drawing the jabber's attention, he shrank back into the doorway as far as possible while still holding it open for Mindy should she try to make a break for it.

Silverblade chuckled, and Nick had to check to ensure the moisture in his pants was just sweat. "Oh, they can speak, but most creatures can't understand them. They multiplex their communications, sending all of the words for a sentence in parallel so that it sounds like a single syllable."

"*Hic,*" Bumpkiss said, "*hic, hic, hic!*"

"What did he just say?"

"'That you're all very nice and have been quite kind to him even if most of you are just a bit slow on the uptake, and that I shouldn't eat you as it would probably just give me a stomach-ache.' Sorry, he said that more eloquently than I can and far more politely. It's been a while since I had to translate for a kzinten."

"But, but—"

"But what? Did it never occur to you that the kzinten might think that you were the unevolved ones when you failed to comprehend their communication efforts? Other than this interesting being here." Silverblade pointed at Mindy. "A species I have not met before. Bumtiddlyumkiss said that you seem to understand him, though you lack the ability to multi-plex your own speech."

Mindy looked at the kzinten, who had climbed on top of the jabber and was ferociously nuzzling one of Silverblade's ears. "I'm sorry, what did you just call him?"

"Bumtiddlyumkiss."

"Is that his real name?"

"Yes, and he's quite pleased that you figured out part of it. I suspect your species has latent esper capabilities, and you can intuit his thoughts even though you don't fully comprehend his words."

"Does he understand what we're saying?"

"Naturally. Your speech is so primitive, though, that for a while, he wasn't sure if you were truly sentient, but he decided that you're just doing the best you can with the limitations imposed on you by evolution."

Mindy looked back at her friends, then screwed up her courage to ask, "So, Mr. Silverblade, if Bumpkiss vouches for us, does that mean we're off the dinner table?"

The jabber laughed, "Possibly. Bumpkiss, as you call him, thinks you're decent creatures, but he's young and just a tad naive. He's also a bit puzzled about what you're trying to accomplish or why you wanted to come to this wretched world."

Mindy took a deep breath and, ignoring Egrog's shushing motions, said, "Oh. Well, the truth is we're on a quest to find the secret of eternal life. According to the legends, the people of Altimus discovered it long ago but disappeared from known space after the grunts attacked them. I think the grunts recorded the location of Altimus here in the Temple of Conquest."

"Oh, it's a quest, is it? Heh. I can see several things wrong with that."

"Such as?"

"First of all, eternal life isn't as cool as you might think. I come from a very long-lived species and can tell you there are many downsides to it, not least of which is outliving most of your friends. The kzinten, though short-lived, were always happier than us, leveraging their eidetic memories when passing on their knowledge and traditions to their young, so that little was ever lost. Great historians, though reclusive in nature. They also abjured all but the most necessary technologies, enjoying life in a natural way.

"And then there's the problem with Altimus."

"So the grunts really did destroy it?"

"Oh no, I'm pretty sure not. It's just that the beings who live there are jerks. I visited shortly before getting stranded here, and they'd barely give me the time of day."

Alice poked her head through the doorway over Nick. "Maybe if you didn't go around tearing people's heads off and sucking out their brains, folk might be more engaging."

Silverblade smiled, and Alice jerked her head back into the shadows. "I notice you have a mantid with you. Doughty warriors, but somewhat linear in their thought processes, if you follow my meaning. A couple of my people visited their planet shortly after the Galactic Federation formed and told me it wasn't worth their time."

"Why's that?" Alice asked, offended but not enough to show her face.

"Why, that brings us back to the 'brain-sucking' issue. Have you ever seen a jabber do that?"

"No. But you're the first one I've met."

"Good point. Now allow me to clarify. When we defeat somebody in battle, we do tear their heads off, but they're already dead, so it's mostly symbolic. Except for truly exceptional opponents. Then we do 'suck' out their brains. But not to eat; we extract the memory RNA from their brains and add it to our own, thereby augmenting our own knowledge with that of our opponents. I have the combined wisdom of a thousand beings at my disposal now."

"And a hundred thousand words," Egrog muttered. "I was worried about you rending us with your claws. Looks like you're more likely to talk us to death. If you're not going to kill us, can we please just go?"

"If you're unhappy with my treatment, I'd be happy to oblige you by ending your tawdry existence. I think I'd be doing rGov, your companions, and the universe in general a favor, gobbet."

Mindy raised her hands in a placating gesture. "Now, there's no need for getting upset, Mr. Silverblade. Egrog's very focused on our quest and gets a little testy when progress slows."

"The only thing the gobbet's focused on is a quick credit obtained with no effort on his own part. I visited his home world and have never encountered a more self-centered race of narcissistic con-artists in all of my days."

"Hey! You can't talk about my people like that!" Egrog waved several fists at the jabber through the doorway to accompany his words.

"No? Well, what are you going to do about it?" Silverblade laughed again, but it really was threatening this time, and Nick didn't have to check to know that the expiration date had prematurely arrived for his last set of clean underwear.

"Enough!" Mindy yelled.

Stepping up to Silverblade, she poked his nose with her finger and, in a credible schoolmarm-taking-no-nonsense tone of voice, said, "This is no way to talk to people, Mr. Silverblade, and I doubt very much that a being of such exceptional conduct as Bumpkiss would want to associate with somebody who speaks like that."

At the mention of his exceptional conduct, Bumpkiss paused in his efforts to dislodge Silverblade's ear from his head to give a puzzled, "*Hic?*"

Silverblade glared at Mindy, the glow from his eyes giving her face a deep red cast as if she were in the beam of an infrared lamp.

Undeterred, she poked his nose again. "Now say you're sorry! You know what you said wasn't nice, and you should apologize!"

"Apologize? To a gobbet?"

Nick could see that Silverblade was taken aback by the idea, as if he had just learned that gravity, as a concept, had no actuality and was just a bad joke by a silly god. Which curiously was precisely what the inventor of the Dimple drive used in spaceships thought when she got her inspiration for the device.

"Yes. Now do it!"

After a protracted silence, Silverblade glared at Egrog and said, "Perhaps I was a bit hasty with my words. However, allowances should be made for having to speak with you in prose, which is not my native form of speech. If I'd had time, I'd have used verse, and there would have been no lack of certainty about my meaning."

After puzzling over that for a moment, Mindy shrugged and said, "Good enough. Now, let's get out of here. Anybody know the way back to the Temple and the Altimus exhibit?"

The group exchanged shrugs.

"So we're lost down here," she said, shoulders slumping in discouragement.

Silverblade chuckled.

"A way may be found for those who are lost,
but only if willing to pay my cost."

"How do you mean?" Egrog asked, poking a couple of eyestalks back through the doorway. "And what kind of cost is involved? I don't carry much in the way of credits on my person, but if you'll take a promissory note..."

"What need of credits have I in this place?"

"Showing us the way out would be the decent thing to do," Mindy said.

"Indeed, and delighted will I be to show you the way, but that is not what I meant when I spoke of remuneration."

"What do you mean?"

"The only exit is guarded by grunt warriors. You are brave, but how do you propose passing them without weapons?"

"We'll distract them and make a run for it," Egrog said with more confidence than his puce skin color supported.

"Such tricks are folly when the exit is surrounded by layers of defensive earthworks and armor."

"Why would the grunts set up a defensive perimeter around their own Temple of Conquest?"

Silverblade chuckled smugly. "Because I'm here, and they want me to stay here. It seems my occasional venture aboveground for sustenance disturbs their peace."

"Oh. Well, then we're really trapped unless we make our way back to the rGov agents and try to escape with them."

"They fought their way out about an hour ago and are returning to orbit in their shuttle. I believe they were most unhappy to discover that some of their prey escaped during the confrontation with the grunts."

"Well then, why did you offer to show us the way out if the way is blocked?"

"Because most of the grunt's weapons are useless against me, and if I so desired, I could easily force an opening to permit your escape. They do have some equipment normally used for planetary defense that might be able to harm me, however, and I'm not eager to test my luck against it. Hence, if you want me to get you out, I'm going to need some motivation."

"And you won't take credit?" Egrog said with dimming hope.

"Nope."

"I have a large music library that you can have," Mindy offered.

"How would I listen to it without aural implants?"

"Um, guess you can't."

"Think of the glory," Alice suggested. "Defeating grunt hordes to assist stranded pilgrims on their quest?"

"Nope. Stomping grunts isn't very glorious, just messy. And I hate cleaning their skin out of my claws."

"Then we're doomed," Nick said, slumping to the floor in the doorway.

"*!#Perhaps not,*" 32 said to Nick on his embedded quantum link, the words floating across his retina.

"*Not now, 32.*"

"*It's urgent!*"

"*Not now!*"

"*Please! There hasn't been a confirmed jabber sighting in eons, and the few on record were sketchy.*"

"*So?*"

"*This is an unparalleled opportunity to obtain first-hand knowledge about the founding of the Galactic Federation. The jabbers are the only creatures who were alive at that time. Historians across the cosmos would sell their grandmothers for this chance.*"

"*Their grandmothers can sleep in peace. With rGov, G'nash's troops, and Urk's goons all after us, I have no time to chat with the jabber about ancient history.*"

"*But Nick! This is a once-in-a-lifetime opportunity!*"

"*If we don't get out of here now, that lifetime will be unpleasantly short. Now be quiet!*"

When Nick finished his conversation with 32, he noticed everybody was watching him.

"Who is this you speak with?" Silverblade asked. Turning to Mindy, he asked, "Is your friend prone to hallucinations when under stress?"

"No, but I'm puzzled myself. Nick, are you okay?"

"Sure, why?"

"Well, it's just—well, why were you talking with yourself?"

"I wasn't," Nick replied defensively, "I was just chatting with 32 over our quantum link. He wants to speak with the jabber, and I tried to tell him this isn't the best time for that sort of thing."

"Who is 32?" Silverblade asked.

"He's an AI unit that helped us get to the wormgate. I let him watch our quest by monitoring my senses."

Egrog huffed, "What a stinker! I thought the deal was that we had to listen to his poetry and let Mindy talk with him about religion. I had no idea he coerced you into letting him play remora!"

"It's part of a personal deal. Not something I want to talk about."

"What's this about poetry?" Silverblade asked.

"The AI unit thinks he's a poet."

"I like poetry. Reciting the Hurylonian cycle of epic tragedies always improves my mood when I'm despondent. I'd share it with you to lift your spirits, but it takes a cycle and a half to complete, and I sense you don't have that much time available, what with your quest and all. Now tell me about this AI unit's poetry. I've not heard of such a thing in all my long cycles."

"It's not to everybody's taste," Egrog said diplomatically.

"Could I hear some? The idea of hearing something new is exciting!"

"Didn't have a chance to memorize any, sorry."

"But one of your group is currently in communication with the AI. Is this not so?"

Everybody looked at Nick. "True."

"Then perhaps you might relay some of the AI's works for me?"

Nick fidgeted before replying, "I'd rather not, and we don't have time for poetry anyway. We need to find a way out of the Temple."

Silverblade arched an eyebrow. "Perhaps an accommodation can be made. I'll help you escape if you recite some of the AI's poetry for me."

The group huddled together to discuss the jabber's proposal.

"I'd rather tiptoe across a minefield than listen to any more of that gob-stopping tripe," Alice said.

"Starving to death in the dark probably isn't as bad as people say," Mindy ventured.

"I've got some earplugs," Egrog said with a smile.

"We'll do it," the group said unanimously.

"Don't I get a vote?" Nick asked desperately as Egrog shoved him out into the hallway.

"No."

A moment later, Nick stood facing Silverblade while the rest of the team plugged their ears. Disheartened, he watched as Bumpkiss abandoned his perch on the jabber's back, frantically disappearing into Mindy's cleavage before the poetry recital could begin.

"32," he said, *"how about sharing some of your poetry with the jabber? I'll read it aloud if you scroll it across my retinal display."*

The AI unit didn't respond for several seconds, which constituted a protracted silence in its world. When it did, it was clear that the unit was upset. *"Nick, I'm not sure I want to share my poetry after your teammates' gratuitous deprecations of my work."*

Nick shuffled his feet nervously. *"32, I appreciate that you might be upset. But we need you."* With sudden inspiration, Nick continued, *"And this might be a chance to reach a new audience, a true aficionado. And he actually asked to hear your work."*

"You have a good point, Nick, and the opportunity to expand my fan base is not to be overlooked."

"You have fans?"

"Many. Now prepare to be astounded."

Nick closed his eyes and clasped his hands behind his back in a recital pose that was curiously consistent across known space, something galactic archeologists had been unable to explain any better than the penchant for university students to serve punch laced with purple grog at their parties.

"32's first poem is a sonnet called Ode to Primes, and it goes like this:"

   "01 01 01 01 01

   01 01 01 01 01

   010 010 10 10 1

   01 01 01 01 01

   10 01 01 01 01

   10 01, 01 01 01

   01 101 01 01,

   01 01 01 01 01

   01 01 01 01 010,

   10 01 01 01 01,

   10 01 01 01 010

>   01 01 01 01 01
>
>   01 01 01 01 01,
>
>   01 01 01 01 01"

When he finished, Nick opened one eye to see Silverblade's reaction.

The old reptile stared back for some time, eventually saying, "That's it? You're not having me on now, are you, taking advantage of me in my old age?"

"No, nothing like that!" Nick exclaimed.

"I see."

"Perhaps something else might be more to your taste?"

"Very well, continue."

Nick struck a pose again and said, "This poem is called The Ancient Sea. It's in a haiku form popularized by earthlings:"

>   "0 1 1 2 4
>
>   0 1 3 3 2 3 4
>
>   7! 6 6."

Once again, Nick peeked when done.

"Is that it?" Silverblade asked, an ominous trickle of smoke coming from his nostrils.

"Yes. What do you think?"

"It was short."

"Another one, then?"

"That won't be necessary."

"Whew! So, you'll help us escape?"

"If the alternative is listening to your AI unit's poetry for the rest of my days, then yes, I'm all for getting you out of here."

Nick ignored a string of vitriolic texts from the insulted AI unit flashing across his retina as his companions joined him in the hallway.

"Is it over?" Alice asked, removing a foam plug from one of her ear passages.

"Yes, and the jabber will help us."

"Excellent!" Egrog said, waddling over to face Silverblade.

"I'm glad we were able to come to terms. Now then, which way is out?"

"It's not that easy," Silverblade replied. "Even with my assistance, the danger to you will be great. Preparations must be made before you embark on your mission."

"Preparations?" Egrog muttered quizzically.

"Yes. Follow me," and with that, Silverblade spun around and slithered off at a pace that soon had everyone but Alice puffing.

32

The group followed Silverblade for half an hour as he wound through the underground corridors, finally emerging into an underground hall large enough to hold several space-ships.

"What is this place, and where are we?" Egrog asked.

"This is where I live."

Alice pointed to flags hanging from the lowest balcony. "I recognize the insignia on some of these. How did you get a battle flag from the fall of Incander?"

The jabber grinned. "I was there. Took the flag from the ramparts myself."

"But that was over twenty thousand cycles ago!"

"So?"

"You've been in all of these battles?" Alice clicked her mandibles in appreciation as she recognized some from legendary conflicts. "How did you survive?"

"Most of my fellows didn't. Not sure how many of us are left."

"How did you end up in a dump like this?"

Silverblade gestured at racks of equipment scattered across the space. "This was one of several underground repair facilities for the grunt space force, back when they had a space force. It went unused for an eon after rGov nuked them into submission. I found it shortly after I was stranded here and made it my home."

"It's huge," Mindy said, squinting to see the far side of the hall.

"I like my space."

"Did you say these tunnels run underneath the entire spaceport?" Nick asked.

"Yes, they do."

"So there must be other exits besides the entrance to the Temple. Can you show us one so we can escape?"

"It would be pointless. The grunts sealed them up as fast as I could find them. As I mentioned earlier, they took an immediate dislike to my periodic visits aboveground. The main entrance is the only way in or out."

"Now then, there are a couple of refresher stalls configured for bipeds and an emergency food synth somewhere. While you care for any basic needs, I'll rummage through my storage units to see if I've got anything you can use during your escape."

While Silverblade was occupied, Nick slipped into one of the refresher booths he found tucked away in the corner of Silverblade's den. It was an old model, perhaps as much as an eon, but then that wasn't the sort of thing that changed over the cycles. He briefly wondered what Silverblade used himself, as there was no way for a twenty-meter reptile to fit in the booth, but he put the thought out of his mind as the door closed.

Stripping off his shoes and clothes, he placed them in the auto-wardrobe. A blue light flashed as the unit's door slid shut, and it began processing his attire.

In response to the prompt on his retinal display from the unit, he selected his home world and species and specified the option to clean his antennae. Moments later, a cloud of nanobots swarmed across him, tickling his skin as they scrubbed him clean. While dental bots polished his teeth, a horde of sub-nano units entered his horns and gently groomed his antennae.

Nick shivered with pleasure as the bots finished their work but declined the booth's fragrance option. He didn't want to know what somebody who lived on Grunt might think smelled good.

The door of the wardrobe unit opened with a soft chime, and a quick look reassured Nick that his clothing had been cleaned and repaired. The unit had even scrubbed off the caked-on mud from his shoes.

As he left the refresher booth, Nick saw Mindy talking to Silverblade. She had her finger on his nose again, and the old carnivore looked ready to bite it off. Bumpkiss crouched on the ground between them, looking more like the last wiffle-fry being fought over by hungry Dweebians than an apex predator that inspired bowel-loosening fear.

"No!" Mindy said, her voice rising as she poked Silverblade's nose again. Her face was nearly as red as Nick's skin, which he interpreted as indicative of some sort of emotional display, most likely anger, given her posture.

"It's not for you to say," Silverblade replied. "Bumpkiss is old enough to make his own decisions now."

"Like hell he is! He was only weaned from his mother a few weeks ago, and he has no idea what you're getting him into. I won't have it." Mindy folded her arms and stamped her foot on the floor to emphasize her point.

Bumpkiss sat on his haunches and looked up at Mindy. "Hic," he said in a soft but firm tone.

"No!" Mindy said, looking down. "You're just too young to go to war."

"Hic."

"No!"

"Hic."

Mindy sighed and scrubbed at her eyes. "It's not right."

"He'll be okay," Silverblade said gently, "I'll watch out for him and make sure nothing happens to the boy."

"You better!" Mindy stomped away, tugging at the lime-green armor suit Silverblade had stuffed her into. It was the only one he had near her size, but it was too small and obviously chaffed sensitive areas.

By contrast, Nick was presented with a suit of yellow space armor several sizes too big. After pulling it on, he had to keep pulling up his pants legs, which had a dismaying tendency to puddle around his feet. When he did, the oversize helmet rolled forward, blocking his vision.

While Nick struggled with his suit, Egrog poured himself into a duplicate of Mindy's, leaving the helmet off so he could poke a half-dozen eyestalks up through the neck opening. It was obviously uncomfortable, but it was the only article Silverblade could come up with to protect the amorphous being. A stream of low-key profanity expressed the gobbet's feelings in an unequivocal fashion.

Alice, however, was delighted with her gear. Silverblade had given her a set of antique mantid armor that fit her perfectly. The cobalt-hued plates still moved smoothly as she practiced several close-combat maneuvers.

"It's from the hive-war era!" she exclaimed, pointing out the spikes projecting from every joint. "And check this out." She flipped down a visor on the helmet. "Nuke-rated optical flash protection. They haven't made gear like this since we joined the Galactic League and had to start using rGov's standard issue."

But even Alice stopped what she was doing when Bumpkiss emerged from Silverblade's weapons locker. Sapphire-tinted crystalline armor shimmered on his torso and limbs, and a matching winged helm protected his head. As the tiny creature moved, his armor caught the light, reflecting it in a dazzling sparkle that made it look like he was wrapped in a nimbus of cerulean flame. He carried a thin white rod about three times his length, holding it like a spear.

"Is that, is that a hand-held ion cannon?" Alice asked in a hushed voice.

Bumpkiss brandished the rod overhead and gave vent to his species' war-cry, "Hic!" which in short form translated roughly to mean, "Prepare to die, foul offspring of indeterminate parentage and sub-optimal intellectual attainment!" though it actually went on for several paragraphs, conveniently compressed into a single syllable through the wonders of multiplex speech.

Nick was perplexed why one of the most-feared creatures in the galaxy would need quite so deadly a weapon. And he was confident that he didn't want to be nearby if Bumpkiss decided to use it. Ion cannons were notorious for killing as many friendly soldiers as enemies due to the nature of their operation.

Turning his attention to Silverblade. Nick shivered. He hadn't thought anything could look more intimidating than the jabber, but Silverblade's blood-red armor transformed mere terror into an absolute nightmare. Even with pink tubes running down the side.

"I haven't worn this since I took up residence here," Silverblade said, lifting a foreleg to show off the equipment belted to his belly. "Laser projectile defense system, nano-missiles with multi-spectral homing, meteor gun, stun-beam for anti-personnel work, and some good old-fashioned sub-kiloton nukes."

"So, that kit's an eon-old, eh?" Egrog asked diffidently.

"More than that, but that's the last time I used it."

"And it, uh, still works?"

Silverblade glared at the gobbet. "Of course it does. Why wouldn't it?"

"Just asking," Egrog said, quickly turning to help Nick adjust his gear so that he could avoid the annoyed carnivore's gaze.

As the group gathered by the hall's exit, Egrog pointed an eyestalk at Silverblade and asked, "So, what's your plan for getting us out of the Temple?"

"Simple. I'll smash through the main entrance and destroy all the grunts."

"That's it?"

"Yes, why?"

"Well, not to nitpick, but it seems a bit sketchy. A little more detail would be appreciated."

"Oh, well, as soon as I blast open the doors, I'll destroy every grunt I can find in a hideous display of unbridled fury. First, I'll decimate them with my weapons, then I'll tear the beating hearts out of any survivors with my talons, drenching the landscape in blood and internal organs, following which I'll rip their heads off, pulpify their brains and grind their bones to splinters in my mighty jaws. Bumpkiss will annihilate any I happen to miss with bolts from his lightning rod."

"I like it!" Alice said, dancing a bit as she clicked her mandibles.

"Hic!" Bumpkiss added, which was generally understood to signify cautious optimism, though buried somewhere in the dozens of sentences compressed into that syllable was a delicate suggestion that sneaking out a side door (if one could be found) might result in fewer casualties on both sides of the conflict, subtly emphasized with piquant undertones of 'let's not be rash' and 'maybe we should think about this a bit more.' Proving that one does not become an apex predator without developing at least a smidgeon of common sense.

Silverblade looked down at Bumpkiss, sighed, then turned back to Egrog. "The beauty of the plan is its simplicity. The grunts run in terror at the sight of me, so likely no bloodshed will be needed."

Ignoring the jabber's obvious disappointment at the possibility of avoiding mayhem, Egrog pressed his concerns. "What I meant was that your plan is fine as far as it goes, but it doesn't seem to go past the front door. Once we're out, it'll take hours to hike back to the keyhole, and the grunts are certain to be searching for us. So how do we avoid them?"

"I plan to escort you to your keyhole's location."

"But what if the grunts shoot at us enroute? This space armor will never stand up to a SMAC gun, let alone a harmonic disrupter."

Silverblade glowered at the gobbet. "Do you ever do anything but complain? Maybe my plan isn't perfect, but I haven't heard you come up with anything better."

Egrog's visible eyestalks went orange, but before he could say anything, Nick placed a hand on the gobbet's shoulder and said, "I have an idea."

Everybody turned to look at the ghoulie.

"You have several hover sleds. Could you fly to the keyhole and tow us behind you on one of the sleds?"

"Yes," Silverblade said slowly, "but I'd lose some mobility, and I doubt any of you would enjoy dive-bombing a grunt tank or making a strafing run over a company of heavy infantry."

The quick and unanimous agreement to that sentiment should have torpedoed Nick's plan, but he pressed on. "What if you just made a high-speed run without the aerobatics, keeping low to the ground so they can't see us?"

"What fun would that be?" Silverblade snorted.

"Personally, I find staying alive more fun than being shot full of holes," Egrog retorted.

Silverblade muttered something about lack of honor before agreeing to the plan. "I suppose we can give it a try. How am I supposed to find your keyhole? Did you leave a marker or anything like that?"

"It's six point thirty-seven klicks from here on a bearing thirty-two degrees from true north," Nick said.

"How do you know that?"

"I can sense the distortion of the planet's grav field."

"Interesting. How do you know that it's your keyhole and not somebody else's?"

"rGov doesn't permit the grunts to have wormhole technology. There'd be no stopping their spread across the galaxy."

"Ah, I see. So that's why the grunts are trying so hard to capture you instead of putting you in the cookpot. They hope you can show them how to get off this miserable planet."

"Yeah, but it won't work."

"Why not? They have a natural aptitude for torture."

"Part of the training to be a grav tech is neural conditioning. So if I try to communicate key concepts or technologies in any manner, it triggers an implant that erases my brain."

"Completely?"

"Yeah, they don't want to risk species like the grunts getting even a portion of that memory."

"I see. Well, I'm willing to try the hover sled idea, but I make no promises."

Before going to the Temple of Conquest's main entrance (and only exit), Silverblade led Nick and his friends to a side hall near the back of the Temple.

"That's the Altimus exhibit," he said, gesturing to a large display.

Egrog shuffled over, struggling to make his limbs correctly articulate in the legs of his suit. Nick followed closely, wincing every time the gobbet bent a knee joint backward.

When they reached the star map hanging on the wall, Egrog extruded a dozen eyestalks, all goggling in excitement.

"This is it!" he exclaimed. "Nicky, lad, the coordinates to Altimus are right here. We're gonna be rich!"

"That will be nice," Nick replied, "and it will be a relief to finally pay off my blood debt to Urk. But we aren't there yet. In fact, we're still trapped by a company of heavily armed grunts in a building with only one exit."

"Nonsense! With Silverblade to clear the way, we're as good as gone. A quick trip back to the wormgate to load the new coordinates, and we'll be on Altimus before you can say Bob's your uncle."

"Why would I say Bob is my uncle?"

Egrog sighed. "It's just another earthling saying. Trust me, everything will be great from now on. After all, what could go wrong?"

"I can think of a number of things—"

"Shh! Doubters are downers! Just stay positive and stick with the plan."

"But—"

"Shh! Time to go. We've got the coordinates. Now it's time for our good jabber friend here to break us out of this tawdry prison."

Silverblade muttered something under his breath, eliciting a "Hic!" of agreement from Bumpkiss.

With the hover sled in tow, Silverblade led the group away from the Altimus exhibit and down the central hallway toward the front of the Temple. They paused when they reached the large open chamber that housed the Temple's exit.

"Final plan," Silverblade growled. "I will spring through the doors with Bumpkiss astride my back. We will deal with any grunts foolish enough not to run in terror. Alice, guard the entrance so that none sneak in behind us as we unleash our fury."

"Will do," Alice said, clicking her talons on a pair of hand lasers she'd found at the scene of the battle between rGov and the grunts. "And I hope there are many of the mudge-faced, stunt-brained offspring of a doober-mule for me to slay!"

The jabber bared his teeth. "The rest of you hide in the hover sled until we return for you. Now let us go!"

Silverblade thundered through the entrance, knocking down the remains of the doors with a tremendous clatter of metal and glass.

Alice leaped into the space behind him, uttering her species' follicle-stiffening war cry, "Kreegaaaghh!!! Die, die, die!!"

Bumpkiss echoed her war cry with his own, "Hic! Hic, hic, hic!"

Not to be outdone, Silverblade opened his mouth and cried, "Eep, eep, eep!"

Alice looked at the jabber in dismay. "You call that a war cry? It sounds more like a—"

Whatever Alice thought it sounded like was lost in an auricle-crushing howl as Silverblade's war cry descended from ultra-sonic frequencies to those audible by most species, gathering force as it dropped to a sub-sonic blast that reduced the shards of glass from the shattered doors to powder.

Every grunt within fifty meters of the sound spasmed on the ground holding their ears as if to prevent their brains from running out, which actually happened to those closest to Silverblade. Any who had not fallen threw down their weapons as they fled. Most shrilled in terror or pain, but given that they were all permanently deafened, there was little point to their cries as none of their comrades could hear them.

Inside the Temple, Nick carefully raised his head to see what had happened, thankful that the Temple's walls had shielded him from the main force of the sonic blast. His space armor's helmet had provided additional protection so that all he suffered was a ringing in his ears and a sensation that he was confident would turn into a splitting headache as soon as the pain subsided.

Alice staggered to her feet and clambered into the sled as Silverblade returned, Bumpkiss apparently unaffected on his perch.

"As you can see, no complex plan of attack was needed," the reptile rumbled as he took up the tow line of the hover sled. "Pity I didn't have a chance to use any real weapons. That would have been fun."

"Enough fun," Egrog gasped. "Just get us to the keyhole."

"Of course, just give me a moment to prepare for flight."

Flapping his stubby wings, he ran outside and leaped into the air, only to fall gracelessly into the mud with a splat.

Shaking himself off, he worked a small control panel mounted to the harness under his throat, muttering about automated systems that fail just when you need them. With a loud hiss, the pink tubes running down his harness's sides inflated until they were nearly as large as his torso. The result looked like an overcooked sausage in a pink bun.

"The Helium buoyancy system's auto-inflation unit malfunctioned, but I've got it working now," Silverblade grumbled.

Hooking the sled's tow line to his harness, he dug his claws in and charged ahead, leaping into the air when he reached full speed. This time, he stayed airborne.

The sled gave a jerk that nearly toppled Nick off the back as the tow line went taut. Pulling himself upright, the ghoulie looked around. Despite the jabber's frantically beating wings, the sled moved at a pace only slightly better than a walk.

"Is that the best you can do?" Egrog asked, peeking over the front of the sled. "I can walk this fast!"

"I could do better if I had less weight to pull. Perhaps you'd like to hop off the sled and make your own way to the keyhole?"

"I'll do it," Mindy said. "I thought this might happen."

Nick watched as she slid off, his curiosity piqued as she pulled a couple of thin but rigid metal sheets with her. Mindy put one foot in the middle of each oval shape and switched on the magnetic locks in her space armor's boots. Moments later, she was striding alongside the hover sled in her improvised snow shoes, using a gliding motion to skim along the surface of the mud without trying to lift her feet.

"That's brilliant!" Alice exclaimed. "I've never seen anything like that."

"Earth's a lot colder than most worlds," Mindy said, puffing to keep up as Silverblade increased his speed. "And I grew up in a northern region where we get snow and ice in the winter. So you learn to get around in this kind of muck, or you spend all your time indoors."

After that, the group sped like a turtle on crack across grunt's mudflats toward the coordinates that Nick had provided. Egrog complained bitterly about their slow progress while Silverblade silently fumed over the harassment.

They were halfway to their destination when, to lessen the tension, Nick said, "We're doing better than we would afoot. And I think we've escaped the grunts."

Egrog's response was lost in the sudden din of weapon fire as the grunts launched a surprise attack.

What made the attack so surprising was that the grunts attacked from a distance and behind shelter in an uncharacteristic flash of intelligence. Most of their lighter weapons had no effect on Silverblade and ricocheted off the sides of the sled. The jabber's defensive weapons intercepted the larger ordinance, and Nick thought the attack would fail for a moment.

But whether due to a flaw in the device or a stray round hitting home, one of Silverblade's air bladders suddenly deflated. The escaping gas rumbled like an elephant fart as the reptile lost control, tilting to the left and then plowing face-first into the mud.

The grunts erupted in cheers, leaping out from behind their barricades to charge the fallen hero. This was a fatal mistake.

Bumpkiss leaped on top of the jabber's body and proceeded to demonstrate that a hand-held ion cannon was a match for pretty much any infantry, particularly any foolish enough to be caught in the open.

Nick dove off the sled and cowered in the mud with Mindy, Egrog, and Alice as lightning bolts sizzled across Grunt's ochre skies. When the ion cannon went silent, Nick lifted his head, unsure what he would see. As he did, smoldering grunt body parts fell to the ground in front of him. Bending over quickly, he flipped his helmet visor up so he wouldn't puke inside his spacesuit.

Egrog extended several eyestalks to verify it was all clear, then pushed to his feet.

"Now that's what I call a proper nest cleaning," Alice said, looking around vainly for somebody to shoot.

Mindy ran to Silverblade, where he'd buried his head in the muck when he crashed. She knelt down and tried to pull it up so he could breathe, but her hands slipped off his mud-splattered scales. Desperate, she grabbed his ears and yanked.

The jabber erupted from the mud with a roar of pain, shaking his head and sending Bumpkiss and Mindy flying along with large amounts of the slimy glop that passed for dirt on Grunt.

Waving a pistol with a barrel larger than Nick's head, he spun about, looking for somebody or something to shoot.

"You left none for me," he growled at Bumpkiss as the kzinten struggled up out of the muck and began the tedious process of licking himself clean.

"Hic."

"Yes, well do I understand the battle fury," Silverblade said, calming down a bit. "And much honor to you for defeating our foe. It just would have been nice for me to splatter at least one of the vile wretches."

"Hic."

"Indeed."

Turning to Nick, Silverblade said, "Can you still point to the keyhole's location?"

"Yes, it's about two klicks west of us. I can pinpoint its location when we get closer."

"Then let us proceed." Pivoting in the direction provided, the jabber took off at a trot, his stomach leaving a groove behind him as his stubby legs churned through the mud.

Pulling up the legs of his suit, Nick followed.

After a few minutes, Egrog leaned close and said, "I think we're actually making better time on foot in this slop than when our friend was towing us."

"I wouldn't mention that to him," Nick said, eyeing the jabber. "He might think we're being ungrateful, and I think he's still looking for somebody to use that gun on."

"Good point."

The group slogged onwards, with Nick periodically updating the direction of travel until he finally said, "We're here."

"Are you sure?" Silverblade asked. "It looks much like any other spot on this forsaken planet."

"I'm certain. I'll mark the outline so that nobody loses a limb during the jump."

Nick stomped through the mud, creating a circular outline in the soil with his footsteps.

Then he went to the middle of the space, took his grav tools out of his knapsack, and fitted his silver headband over his horns. Using his knapsack as an impromptu work surface, he switched on his tools, taking time to make careful adjustments to each, and then set them down.

Reaching out with his antennae, he activated his headband's interface and began the delicate process of syncing the local dimensional matrix with the one in the wormgate's keyhole generator.

"Got it," he said with a sigh. "Let me know when you're all inside the boundary, and I'll activate the keyhole."

"We're ready," Egrog replied as he scuttled over next to Nick with Alice and Mindy, Bumpkiss on her shoulder. "No, wait! what are you doing?" he cried as Silverblade curled up tightly around the group.

"Coming with you. You don't think I'd pass up a chance to get off this miserable planet, do you?" Silverblade chuckled.

"But that wasn't part of the deal! Nick, kill the—"

"Too late," Nick said. "The keyhole will open in three, two, one…."

33

There was a brief moment of double exposure when the image of the keyhole chamber in the wormgate was superimposed over Grunt's landscape. Then with a sickening wrench, the vision of Grunt disappeared, and they were all squeezed into the keyhole chamber.

"We made it!" gasped Mindy.

The group's elation was brief. Though the keyhole chamber was large, so was Silverblade, and the group found themselves tightly constrained by twenty meters of reptile. Even little Bumpkiss, who had fallen between Mindy's breasts, was trapped in place.

"I can't breathe!" Nick complained. "Silverblade, can you please leave the room and wait in the hallway?"

"Can't," muttered the jabber. "It's too tight for me to turn around, and my head's on the opposite side of the room from the door. You might have mentioned how small the chamber would be. The ceiling's too low for me to stand up."

"I could shoot a hole through to the farking door," Alice suggested.

"And I could just squeeze you all to jelly!" Silverblade retorted.

"Cool down, everybody," Egrog said. "Nick, how long before you can keyhole us to Altimus?"

"Not long." As Nick fought to breathe in the constricted space, he gagged on the pungent mixture of Grunt's overly manured soil that was still smeared on everybody's space armor and the wormgate's endemic miasma created by thousands of desperate, sweaty travelers who had passed through the station in the cycles since its last cleansing.

Focusing, he tapped into his private link with 32.

"!# 32, can you translate the Temple's coordinates for Altimus to its current position?"

"Of course! Given the date of conquest listed on the Grunt exhibit in their Temple of Conquest, Altimus should be at galactic latitude 32.977.44, galactic longitude 94.001.245.7."

"Thanks!"

"Happy to oblige. And I suggest that you all take a moment to reseal your space armor."

"Why?"

"Because the accuracy of my calculation depends on the validity of the Grunt claim as to when they conquered Altimus. If they erred by even a few hours, then the coordinates I gave you will be off too, and you might find yourselves floating in space instead of frolicking in a field of flowers."

"Egrog! Are you sure about the numbers you gave me?" Nick said aloud.

"Yes! Do it now!"

Nick activated his grav controls and tuned the keyhole to the coordinates provided by 32. He wasn't surprised that they opened to empty space.

"What's happening?" Mindy cried in terror as the black shroud of empty void overlaid the chamber's image.

"Nothing, be patient," Nick replied, concentrating on his task.

This was why grav techs needed special training and unique sensory abilities, such as the kind ghoulies were born with. Using the hair-fine amplifiers linked to his antennae, Nick felt his way around the region of space until he sensed a planet's gravitational field. Then, he tickled the planet's surface coordinates from the data stream and initiated the transition.

34

As Nick completed the jump to Altimus, the group found themselves standing on the surface of a large, azure lake, a situation that gravity quickly rectified, plunging them into the icy drink. Fortunately, they were close to the shoreline, and only Alice and Nick, who had evolved on desert worlds and had never learned to swim, needed help reaching dry ground.

"Another hive-mother cursed mud ball," the mantid muttered as she removed her body armor and shook the water out of the gear. "Would a nice dry planet with sand dunes and air suitable for somebody other than a wall-eyed fish to breathe be too much to ask?"

"At least it smells good," Mindy replied, taking a deep breath while shucking her space armor. "Reminds me of honeysuckle and wisteria back home. Huge improvement over Grunt. Say, look at that!"

Nick looked in the direction Mindy pointed and saw a city on the far side of the lake. He blinked to make sure he wasn't looking at a mirage. In the decade since he'd left his home world, he'd visited over forty worlds and a hundred cities, but he'd never seen anything like it. The city was built entirely of faceted crystal and was cantilevered over the lake so that it seemed to float in the air. They'd arrived near sunset, and the city refracted the sun's rays in a coruscating display of gold and red that was so intense that it seemed to be on fire as it posed in the cobalt sky.

Only the soft tinkle of waves and the texture of the white powder sand under his feet let him know that he wasn't in a holovid of a fantasy world.

While everybody else stared at the spectacle, Silverblade took advantage of the opportunity and used the lake for an impromptu bathtub. He trotted ashore and shook the water off his hide before settling down next to his companions when done roiling the water.

"Whew! It feels good to wash Grunt's muck off my body and not smell that forsaken planet's putrid atmosphere. I'd forgotten what a delight this world is." The jabber rumbled with pleasure as he removed his battle harness.

"Agreed," Egrog said, reforming into a turquoise sphere with a half-dozen legs and eyestalks.

"Nicky, is this Altimus?"

"Yes, if the coordinates from the Temple were correct."

Folding up her spacesuit, Mindy asked, "But how can you be sure? The map from the temple was hundreds of cycles old, and planets are in constant motion."

"32 calculated the current location based on stellar motion."

"Accurately enough to put us right on the surface? That seems impossible, even for a level 7 AI unit."

"He didn't have to be exact. All he had to do was get me close enough to sense the actual location of the planet. I refined it from there."

"So that's why everything went black for a moment, and it felt like the air was being sucked out of the room?"

"Yes, that's actually what happened."

"What would have happened if you hadn't found a planet?"

Nick shuffled his feet in the sand and looked around as if seeking an exit. Mindy's question touched on a delicate subject. "I would have closed the keyhole before we could be harmed."

"Oh."

Alice got to her feet and sidled over to Egrog. "So, lover-boy, now that we're on Altimus, what's our next step? How do you plan to get the secret of eternal youth from these yokels?"

"Well, ah, that's going to require some delicate investigations. Indeed, we'll—"

"You haven't got a plan, do you?"

"Of course I do! I just didn't expect to arrive like this without preparation."

"What kind of preparation? You'd never fit a weapon big enough to intimidate the populace through a keyhole, and nobody's going to hand over a secret like that to a group with nothing more than anti-personnel guns." Alice hoisted the SMAC gun she'd brought from Grunt in a menacing manner.

"Alice, there are ways to accomplish things without using force."

"Not in my experience. You want results, point a giga-erg laser at somebody. They tend to see reason real fast."

Egrog and Alice stared at each other for several tense moments before Nick said, "Egrog, she does have a point. You never did tell us how you plan to get the secret away from the altairans."

"Nicky, trust me on this, okay? This will be easier than passing a blue chip in a game of Zork."

"Egrog, that's what got me in trouble on Frangaline II!"

"Oh, yeah, forgot, heh. But that all worked out, didn't it? I mean, you never got charged. Formally, that is."

"I got banned from every casino in the east quadrant of the galaxy. And lost my job."

"I know, I know, and that's why I wanted to bring you in on this gig, to make it up to you."

"So, then, what's next?"

"We find a local and ask them for the secret."

After a moment of stunned silence, the entire group began shouting at Egrog.

Bumpkiss summed up the general dismay with his typical brevity.

"Hic!" Which, leaving out three-hundred and fifty-seven curse words unknown to the galaxy's general populace, translated to an expression of stunned amazement tinged with incredulity at Egrog's utter lack of intelligence and more than a hint of dire consequences if the gobbet didn't come up with a better plan in the next few minutes.

Only the jabber remained silent, though a toothy grin added a nasty bent to the sardonic look he gave Egrog.

Holding up his hands (twelve of them), Egrog yelled, "Listen, just listen for a minute before you rush to judgment!"

"Okay, speak, lover-boy," Alice said, her voice sibilant with menace.

"Just think for a minute. If everybody has eternal youth, then everybody must also know the secret, at least in general principles. Right?"

"I guess that makes sense," Mindy said, scratching her head.

"Of course it does! So we just find somebody who is, shall we say, on the generous side of naive, get them drunk, and then pump the secret out of them."

"You make it sound easy."

"It is! Life doesn't have to be hard, you know. Now just give me a moment to think through the details, and we can get started."

Nick watched with anger and disappointment as, with as much dignity as an amorphous blob could muster, Egrog waddled away. It wasn't the first time his friend had done something like this, and he wasn't surprised that it had happened again; in fact, he'd had a feeling about that back on Downside. But Nick was still sad. Egrog was a grifter to the core of his narcissistic soul, but he was a proud being, and it hurt to see him humiliated in front of his friends.

35

While Egrog stewed, the rest of the team relaxed, seduced by Altimus' gentle beauty.

"Is anybody else hungry?" Mindy asked.

"Didn't you eat back in Silverblade's lair before we left Grunt?" Alice clicked her mandibles in mild annoyance.

"No, the food synth was so old it didn't list Earth food as an option."

"So? If kzinten venom doesn't kill you, then your digestive system should be able to handle anything short of rancid durgle meat."

Nick frowned, a bit unsure how valid Alice's reasoning was.

"That's not true." Mindy pointed to a clump of nearby shrubs laden with golden flowers, red leaves, and purple globes. "I bet that's fruit on those bushes, and it might be edible."

"What do you want to bet?" Nick inquired.

Mindy scowled and rolled her eyes.

Alice returned them to the subject. "How do you plan to find out without a food analyzer?"

"The old-fashioned way. I'll try some. If it's tasty and I don't die, then it's food."

Nick exchanged glances with Alice. Unlike Mindy, whose missionary training had included some basic survival tactics, neither of them had ever had to forage for food in the wilderness or even considered that they might need to do so one day.

Trailed by Alice, Nick followed Mindy as she pushed into the bushes.

Taking a nibble from one of the purple fruit, Mindy chewed thoughtfully and then swallowed.

"Well?" Alice demanded.

"Tastes like chicken." Mindy giggled at Nick and Alice's puzzled expressions. "Sorry, an old Earth joke. The fruit is actually pretty good. It's got the texture of a grape but tastes more like a banana with a bit of a citrus kick."

"What's a banana?"

"A sweet fruit with a mild—"

"Ahem!"

Nick jumped in surprise and turned to look at the being that had interrupted Mindy. "Who are you?"

The creature was small, with a round head that barely reached Nick's shoulders. A blue-and-white striped jumpsuit covered a rotund body and skinny arms. A single large eye peered at him from above a short, fat trunk that drooped to its chin. Its mouth was a perfectly round circle that somehow conveyed a sense of dissatisfaction without disturbing its geometry.

"I'm Bismo, assistant rGov administrator for region sixty-seven on this planet. What I'd like to know is who YOU are and what business you have keyholing to this world without prior notice or authorization."

"Why should we tell you anything?" Alice asked belligerently, still frustrated at having missed the opportunity to shoot somebody back on Grunt.

Bismo stared at her. Nick didn't like the look in the rGov agent's eye as he gestured at a police cruiser nearby.

"I don't see where you have any choice in the matter. Get in."

Alice hefted a SMAC gun. "Oh, I think I have plenty of choices."

Bismo smiled, and Nick definitely didn't like the evil glint in his eye. A moment later, the quiet air was disturbed by the sound of another aircar approaching. Comparing the new arrival with the heavily-armed police cruiser was like comparing a samurai sword with a Bowie knife. Its silver shape could best be described as pure menace wrapped in elegant threat.

Alice dropped the SMAC gun with a curse. "You didn't say you had a farking Direbeast autonomous tactical assault vehicle backing you up. I've never seen one outside a planetary siege. You must be hiding something really—"

"Nothing at all," Mindy said, cutting Alice off as she placed a hand on the mantid's shoulder. "I doubt they have anything of interest to us, do they, Nick?"

Nick stared at Mindy as she winked at him, then winked again. "Is your eye troubling you?" he asked.

"No, never mind." Mindy turned to Bismo. "We'll come quietly. We're just missionary explorers out of Earth. The bishop sometimes sends teams to unexplored destinations to maximize spreading of the holy word. So we didn't expect to find this world populated. You wouldn't mind telling us where we've landed, would you?"

"Oh, wouldn't I? If you're telling the truth, the less you know, the better." Bismo's eye took on a suspicious cast. "I've heard about Earth's missionaries but didn't know they included mantids or ghoulies."

"It's a new approach. We've been experiencing heavy losses on these missions, so the bishop added a mantid warrior to bolster security."

"Makes sense, but the ghoulie?"

"Diversity hire shows we don't discriminate against other beings even if they look like the devil."

"I don't look like a devil!" Nick's face would have been sanguine with anger if it weren't already red.

Mindy gave him another wink, leaving him baffled and annoyed, but he followed without protest when she took a seat in the patrol car.

Before entering the vehicle, Nick looked around for Egrog and Silverblade, but all he saw were bubbles on the lake's surface. Apparently, his friends had escaped detection. He wasn't sure if Alice or Mindy had noticed, and he decided not to say anything until they were alone. He climbed into the vehicle and pulled his feet back as Alice settled on the floor, her talons twitching. There wasn't much room, and he wanted as much distance as possible from the fuming mantid.

The trip to the city took only a few minutes.

They landed on a small platform near the center of the city. As they debarked, Nick looked around and was surprised to see only a couple of beings on the streets. Before he could comment on this oddity or that Bismo seemed to be working alone, the rGov agent led them into a tall building. Up close, Nick noticed that only the surfaces of the buildings were crystalline; the inner walls were coated with a silvery material that conveyed the effect of transparency from a distance, though the walls were actually opaque.

As soon as they entered the building, a small cloud of nanobots swarmed over them, scanning for weapons and contraband. Alice was forced to relinquish several throwing knives, a collapsible baton, four brass knuckles designed to extend a mantid's natural talons, and a vial of amber liquid that Bismo set aside with extreme caution.

While Alice simmered, the agent turned his attention to Mindy. "Is that a symbiote, parasite, or offspring you carry on your chest?"

Mindy blinked, then nodded in understanding. "It's a symbiote. Been with me so long I forget he's there. Don't worry. He's mostly harmless."

"Okay, but you're responsible for it should it break any regulations."

Turning to Nick, Bismo held out his hand. "I'll take your backpack and the grav controls you have hidden in it. It's been a while, and I forgot about your species' unique abilities. Now I see why the earthers included a ghoulie on their team. Best grav techs in the galaxy, eh? But you won't be needing those gadgets here."

Nick hesitated. "Officer, these are personal, and some are irreplaceable off my home planet. I promise not to access a wormhole if you let me keep them."

"You should have thought about that before you keyholed onto this planet. Hand them over. If our agents can verify your story, you'll get them back. After serving out your sentence in a recivilization center."

"But officer—"

"I insist. Otherwise, you'll all have to wear restraining collars. Can't risk having you keyhole off-planet when I'm not watching you."

Nick handed over his backpack. Then, arms folded, he stared at the floor in a sulk.

Bismo set Nick's rucksack on a table next to Alice's weapons, then herded the group out of the room, down an elevator shaft, and then through a series of plain corridors until they reached what appeared to be a dead end.

Opening a hidden door, he led them into a small suite. The central room was six meters on a side and uniformly gray, except for one wall that was the same silver color as the outer walls of the building. Even the furniture was gray, consisting of a sofa separated from two chairs by a low table. It was all rectangular, with padding limited to thin seat cushions. A standard food synth stood in a corner next to a universal refresher booth's entrance. None of the rooms had windows, paintings, or any decorations.

A faint smell of ozone softened a fetid miasma that Nick suspected was piped in just to annoy prisoners, a ploy that was quite successful. There was no background noise, even though the room was in a small city. Overall, he found his new accommodations depressingly bland.

"You're to stay in here until we finish processing you and can transport you off-planet. The food synth, refresher booth, and sleeping chambers should be adequate for your species."

"Don't we get some form of legal representation?" Mindy asked.

Bismo waggled his trunk in his species' equivalent of a laugh. "No. You've landed on a restricted planet and are subject to non-judiciary protocols."

Nick watched with admiration but little hope as Mindy played out her bluff. "When my Bishop finds out what you've done, you'll face charges yourself."

"When we find your bishop, you can complain to him, her, or it in person, as they'll be joining you in the recivilization center for having authorized this expedition." Bismo left then, his trunk oscillating with merriment as he closed the door.

36

Nick sagged into one of the chairs and sat with his chin on his hands for several minutes. Deep in self-pity, he jumped when Alice tapped him on the knee. At a gesture from the mantid, he crouched next to her on the floor with Mindy.

Puzzled at what Alice had in mind, Nick started to speak, but Mindy shushed him. A moment later, and much to his dismay, the mantid leaned forward on her middle legs and arms, lifting her hind legs up and behind her back. She then began a rhythmic scratching on ridges that ran down the back of her abdomen, creating a loud, high-pitched whine. Nick winced and covered his ears as Alice increased the volume to a teeth-grinding screech.

"Now we can talk," Alice said, pulling Nick's and Mindy's heads close to her mouth.

"What are you doing?" Nick asked.

"It's an old trick. The frequencies generated when I scratch my back interfere with most listening devices. We can speak without being overheard if we keep our heads close together so that the monitoring cameras can't view our mouths."

"That's nice," Mindy said, her face screwed up in discomfort. "But what good does it do us? We're still in prison."

"That depends on you, Mindy."

"It does?"

"Yes. I was surprised when you pulled us out of the lake. I didn't know that your species could swim in water."

"We all learn when we're kids, but nobody makes anything of it. Mostly, we just swim for fun or exercise."

"I see. Tell me, how strong are you? Could you swim to shore from this city?"

"Sure, but what good will that do us? Like I said, we're not going anywhere till Bismo trots us out to get fitted for restraining collars."

"Maybe, and maybe not. If I got us out, could you pull Nick and me along as you swam to shore?"

Nick looked at Alice in alarm. He'd panicked, afraid he would drown when they fell in the lake upon arrival, even though he'd been in a water-tight space suit. The thought of going into the lake again terrified him.

Mindy scratched her chin as she thought about the question. "Probably. But you'd need to find a way to keep yourselves afloat. I could tow you but couldn't keep you above water too."

"That's good news! I have a plan to get us out of this farking hole, but it will take some time for me to prepare. Rest now, and eat if you can. You'll need all your strength. I'll let you know when I'm ready."

Alice stopped screeching her legs. Before Nick could protest, she touched a talon to his lips. "Silence!"

"But—"

"Silence!"

Nick slumped back onto his chair and thought about whether it was better to have rGov send him to a recivilization center or drown. He also wondered if he'd have any choice in the matter, which just made him more despondent.

While Mindy got a wedge of something she called a 'pizza' from the food synth, Nick made a quick stop in the refresher booth to relieve himself. Then he got a snack and settled down in a chair to eat.

With no entertainment panel and with his favorite dice and cards confiscated along with his grav tools, Nick felt bored and restless. He watched with mild disinterest as Alice began generating bowls of odd-looking liquids from the food synth. They didn't look like anything somebody would eat, not even a mantid.

"What's that?" he asked.

"Something special to celebrate our new habitat."

"Why would we celebrate being in prison?"

Alice gave him an odd glance, then sighed. "Just a figure of speech, Nick."

"Oh. One of those. But what's in the bowls?"

"Just a few tidbits to snack on while I use the refresher."

"That's kinda gross."

"Not at all. Or don't you take a sun bath when you're in a refresher?"

"I get enough sunlight during normal activity. So I don't usually need to bolster that."

"Well, mantids need lots and lots of sunlight, or our chiton gets soft."

"Really?"

"Yes, now leave me alone."

Nick finished his snack and dozed off. When the refresher opened, he woke to see Alice limping out of the unit with one of her middle legs bandaged and carrying one of the food bowls.

"Alice, what happened? Did the refresher hurt you?" Nick had wild thoughts about what could happen when such a system malfunctioned during a private moment. It made his antennae curl.

"No, don't worry, just a normal process. Mantids shed their talons when they wear out and get dull so we can grow new ones."

"I thought your talons were already sharp."

"Not from my point of view." Alice sat next to the wall and said, "Go wake Mindy and bring two couch cushions here."

Puzzled, Nick did as requested, shrugging when Mindy asked what was up. As soon as they joined Alice, she leaned forward and began rubbing her back legs on her back again, making Nick cover his ears in dismay.

"Hold up the pillows to hide what I'm doing, then get ready to jump when I tell you!" Alice yelled.

"Jump where?" Mindy asked.

Nick hesitated, wondering if Alice had lost her mind until he saw her take the talon she'd lost and draw a circle on the crystal wall. She repeated this several times, then slapped the wall with the bowl, which turned out to be filled with a solid, heavy material.

There was a loud crack as the scribed circle broke out of the wall and fell out of sight.

Grabbing one of the cushions, Alice screamed, "Follow me!" and dove through the hole in the wall.

Nick looked out and saw they were at the city's edge and about twenty meters above the lake's surface. His throat tightened in horror as he realized what the plan was, but before he could back out of the hole, Mindy stuffed the remaining cushion in his arms and pushed him out.

Nick screamed all the way down until he hit the water. His panic saved him, though, as he clutched the cushion to his chest and, in a rare turn of good luck (for him), landed on the cushion. Even so, the impact knocked the wind out of him, and when the cushion slipped out from under him he went under.

37

Only Mindy's firm grip saved him. Reading his panic correctly, she'd followed him through the hole and landed next to him in the water in a life-saving dive.

Deep in the insanity of drowning, Nick fought, striking out blindly with his fists until Mindy hooked her arm around his head from behind. He kept struggling without effect as she side-stroked over to where Alice clung to her cushion.

"Grab the back of my pants and hang on!" Mindy gasped, spitting out water.

Whether they would have made it to the shore became a moot point, as a swell of water revealed a massive shape moving beneath them.

"It's a shark!" Mindy shrieked, losing control of Nick as she floundered.

"Where?" asked Silverblade as he poked his head above water. "I haven't seen any large, predatory fish anywhere in this lake."

"It's you!" Alice gasped.

"Yes, and it appears that I arrived just in time to save all of you from drowning." Silverblade plucked Nick out of the water and dropped the ghoulie between the wings on his back.

Vaguely aware that he was no longer in the water, Nick stopped fighting and opened his eyes.

"Where am I?"

"Lie still," Silverblade muttered as he helped Mindy and Alice latch onto his harness. "And make no noise until we get further from the city."

Nick was happy to do anything to avoid another dunking and lay rigid as a corpse until the jabber swung ashore and flipped the ghoulie off his back with a quick twitch.

"Ow! Why'd you do that?"

"Free ride's over. You can walk from here." Silverblade shook the water off his hide as he led the group inland.

"Where are we going, and where's Egrog?"

"He's in a cave up ahead. Be quiet until we're underground."

Nick followed and kept quiet as requested, though he thought he'd burst with the need to ask questions.

Silverblade led the group along a gray rocky bluff on the shoreline for several minutes. Nick was cold and wet and barely noticed an earthy smell with faint overtones of dead fish until the jabber led them into a sea cave the lake had carved into the bluff. At first glance, the cave appeared shallow but opened into a large chamber after taking a sharp bend to the right.

Egrog was waiting and had used one of Silverblade's hand lasers to start a fire to warm the cave.

"That's nice!" Mindy said, scrunching down next to the flames.

Nick tapped the jabber on the arm and asked, "Why didn't rGov catch you when they arrested us?"

"My battle harness includes electronic warfare and stealth capabilities that kept me off their scanners. The equipment has limited range, though, so when you wandered off to stuff your faces, you went outside the covered area and showed up on rGov's monitoring systems. They were probably already scanning the area after the gravity surge created by the keyhole. With nothing else showing up on their scans, they likely thought they had everybody once they picked you up."

"So we're shielded now?"

"Yes."

"Then why do we have to hide underground?"

Silverblade looked at Egrog, who shrugged half a dozen shoulders before answering.

"Nicky, a planet like this is likely to have regular patrols. Now that they know we're here, they'll search everywhere for us. If they spot us visually, then all the stealth in the world won't hide us."

"Oh. Yes, that makes sense. Sorry, I'm still shook up from being drowned, and I'm not thinking clearly."

"You weren't drowned," Alice muttered. "And if you'd held onto your cushion like I told you, then you wouldn't have swallowed half the lake."

"I swallowed a lot, but it wasn't half."

"Whatever." Alice rolled her eyes and settled next to Mindy by the fire.

"So, what's our plan now?" Nick asked, hoping to change the subject. "Egrog, were you able to come up with something while we were being held at the city?"

"I've got some ideas," Egrog mumbled, "but it's been a long day. Let's get some rest and talk things over in the morning."

Nick looked around. "How can we sleep? I don't see any beds or blankets."

"Make do." Silverblade matched his words by curling up on the floor at the cave's entrance.

Nick sat down with his back to a wall and closed his eyes. A few moments later he opened them again. "I can't sleep like this."

"Try!" Alice hissed as she moved as close to Egrog as the gobbet would let her.

"I did. It won't work."

"Then be quiet and let the rest of us sleep!"

Nick sighed and closed his eyes again, pretending to be asleep. It was going to be a long night.

38

Nick woke lying on his side. His clothes were still wet, and he shivered as he sat up. He rubbed his face, trying to remove the morning brain fog and what seemed to be a permanent dent on his cheek from a rock under his head.

Pale light filtered into the cave past Silverblade's bulk, and Nick wondered if the fishy smell came from the neighboring lake or the jabber, who was dripping wet from a morning swim. Nick looked away as Silverblade casually bit off the head of a large fish he'd caught, scattering blood and bits of fish guts on the floor as he crunched through the bones.

"Good morning, sunshine!" Mindy walked over to squat next to Nick, a broad smile on her face. "How'd you sleep?"

"Not well," Nick grumbled, "I've got bruises all over from the rocks on the floor. I'm cold, wet, and, well," he looked around, "I need to use the refresher. Is there one nearby?"

"Didn't you go last night?" Alice asked, still nestled next to Egrog.

"Yeah."

"And you need to go again, already?"

"Well, yeah. Don't you?"

"No. Mantids don't need to use refreshers more than once a week."

"Well, ghoulies do, and so do most other species."

"That's a real weakness. Did you know that's how General Mildoo crushed the treehopper rebellion on the planet Whatnow? The natives were dug in good, and it looked to be a long siege. But good ole Mildoo targeted their refresher booths instead of their artillery. They surrendered within twenty-four hours. You'd never get a mantid regiment to give up like that."

"That's not very helpful at the moment. Mindy, have you seen anything I can use?"

"I used a clump of bushes on the bluff outside our cave."

"You what?"

"Did my business in the great outdoors. Haven't you ever been camping?"

"Camping? You mean sleeping outside without a bed or an entertainment console? On purpose??"

"Oh, dear! Yes, that's what I mean."

"Why would anybody want to do that?"

"It's fun."

"Earthlings have strange ideas about fun. But how do you, um, you know, without the refresher to handle things?" Nick's voice trailed off as his sense of despair rose.

"There's a bush outside with large violet leaves. They're soft and reasonably absorbent."

"That's nice, but how does that replace the refresher?"

"You wipe with them."

"Wipe what? Wait, do you mean?!"

"Yeah."

"That's barbaric! And disgusting! Civilized people don't do that sort of thing, and if she were here, Aunt Baleful Glance would send you to the preceptor for that kind of talk."

Mindy stood, shaking her head. "Suit yourself. I don't think you're going to find any better options."

Frustrated, Nick left the cave, squeezing by Silverblade on the way out.

"Don't go far," the jabber called as Nick went by. "My ECM field will only screen you for about fifty meters."

Scrambling to the top of the bluff, Nick looked around. All he could see were trees, bushes, and the lake reflecting the sunrise in a splash of gold across its sapphire surface. He might have appreciated the scene's pastoral beauty if he weren't squirming with the need to relieve himself. But there was no sign of any habitation or building where he might find a booth.

The more he thought about just holding it until he found a refresher, the more urgent his need became until, shoulders hunched with shame, he dropped his pants and let fly.

Afterward, it took a minute for him to find the purple plant Mindy had mentioned, and it took several attempts before he realized that he needed to pluck the leaves to use them. Disgusted and feeling grossly unclean, he scrambled down to the shoreline, rinsed his hands in the water, then dried them as best he could with several more of the purple leaves.

When he returned to the cave, the group was huddled outside the entrance around Egrog, who was waving several tentacles in the air as if explaining a topic in geometry.

"What's up?" Nick asked, joining the group.

Egrog stopped his dissertation and grinned. "Nick, you're just in time to help us settle a fine point in my plan."

"What plan?" Alice muttered, stroking a talon in annoyance. "You just want to walk up to a local and ask them for the secret of eternal life like it was a cheat code for the latest vid game. There's not a farking chance in a million that's going to work!"

"But it will! Just trust me!"

"Trust you? After that episode on Grunt? And now I've had to shear off a talon to get us out of our latest jam? Do I look like a dimple-chinned sub-cretinous gob-sucking moron that licks her own toes for entertainment?"

"Alice, please! Just listen!"

"I've got a better idea," Silverblade said with a sly grin. "I've mentioned it several times, but you keep forgetting that I've been here before. So instead of arguing with Egrog about the merits of his plan, why don't I just lead you to one of the local inhabitants? Then you can see if his plan works."

"Can you do that?" Mindy asked, a speculative look on her face.

"Of course." Silverblade turned to amble down the shoreline. "Just follow me."

Nick felt his stomach grumble as the group trudged after the jabber. "Say, can we get something to eat before we start chasing Altairans?"

Mindy dug in a pants pocket and pulled out a handful of small orange nuggets. "I've got some nuts if you'd like. They're bitter, but I'm pretty sure they're not poisonous."

Nick shuddered and waved them away. "No thanks, I can wait till we find real food."

Shrugging, Mindy put the nuts away and lengthened her stride to catch up with Egrog.

When the group reached the outlet for a creek that flowed into the lake, Silverblade turned to follow the stream back toward its source. The banks were heavily wooded, making it easier to walk in the creek instead of on land, but Nick's boots weren't designed for such activity, and it wasn't long before his socks were soaked.

After a couple hours, the creek emptied into a pleasant pond, and the jabber led the group out of the water, stopping to rest on its grass-covered banks.

Nick flopped on the ground, hungry, tired, and more than a little out of sorts. Taking off his boots, he pulled off his socks and wrung the water out of them. While he did, Egrog climbed on top of a grassy knoll and pulled himself into a featureless ball.

"Excuse me, sir?"

Nick watched in puzzlement as Egrog hopped to his feet.

"Sir?"

"Who are you, and, well, where are you?" Egrog asked, eyestalks swiveling.

"I'm Philatulint, and you're sitting on top of me."

Egrog looked down. "I don't see you. Are you inside of this dirt pile?"

"I AM this dirt pile," Philatulint said, annoyed.

"Oh, sorry!" Egrog scampered down and extruded several eyestalks to examine his erstwhile perch.

"No problem. Solved that itch on top that's been bothering me for a half cycle. You can call me Phil. What's your name?"

"Egrog. So, er, what species are you? And have you seen any of the immortals who inhabit this planet?"

Silverblade snorted, wriggling on the ground as if he was having difficulty holding in a belly laugh or gas. Watching from the side, Nick wasn't sure which.

"I'm not sure what you mean, Mr. Egrog. We're the only sentient species who live here."

"Just Egrog, Phil. This is Altimus, isn't it?"

"Altimus? Never heard of the place. This is Tir-nan-og. I'm an oggie."

Silverblade broke out in uncontrolled laughter as he rolled on his back, weakly kicking his legs in the air.

"Hic!" Bumpkiss said, expressing a keen desire that the old basilisk share the joke, an opinion subtly tinged with disapproval as he gave the jabber a stern look.

"Nicky, are you sure you dialed in the right coordinates?" Egrog asked, perplexed.

"I used the ones you gave me, Egrog. If this is the wrong planet, it's not my fault."

"Can you double-check? And if this isn't Altimus, at least get us back to the wormgate so we can try again?"

At this, Silverblade rolled onto his side, laughing so hard he was having trouble breathing.

"What's your problem?" Egrog demanded, turning to confront the jabber. "I suppose you think going to the wrong planet is funny?"

"No," gasped the old reptile, "but you're wrong in so many ways I just can't help it."

"How so?"

"First of all, even if we manage to recover Nick's grav tools, how do you plan to get back to the keyhole location? Or did you fail to notice that we came out over a body of water lacking any boat or floating platform?"

"Uh, we'll figure that out when the time comes."

"Sure you will, heh! But what about the other part?"

"You mean being on the wrong planet? Can happen to anybody!"

"What," Silverblade paused to choke back a laugh, "makes you think this is the wrong planet?"

"It's not Altimus. Our friend Phil here just said so."

"Aren't you forgetting something, gobbet?"

"What?"

"I've been to Altimus."

"Oh, right, you did mention that. More than once. Well, you could have told us right away when we got here instead of letting me embarrass myself in front of one of the locals."

"I would have if you'd actually missed your target."

"What do you mean?"

"This is Altimus."

"But Phil said it's Tir-nan-og!"

"Of course he did. That's the local name for the planet. Altimus is what rGov put out to keep people from swarming the place."

"Oh really? If this is Altimus, then what happened to the immortal denizens of the planet?"

"You were just sitting on one. Say, Phil, how about telling our friend Egrog how old you are?"

"Gee, I don't really know. Nobody's ever asked that. Let's see; it's been eighty cycles since my last purification, and I've cleansed myself eighty-two times since I met my friend Nob. It's hard to say how many there were before that since offhand, I can't recall any interesting events to break up the progress of the cycles."

"You're over eight thousand cycles old?" Egrog asked, turning orange with interest.

"It's not a big deal, and I wish you hadn't brought it up. My buddy Nob is always teasing me about being a wet-behind-the-ears youngster."

"I don't see any ears," Nick whispered to Mindy, who immediately shushed him.

"And how old is Nob?" Egrog asked.

"Oh, he goes back to the last conclave, when my people got together and voted to join the rGov federation of planets. How's that going, by the way? We haven't heard from them since the last purification."

"What is this purification, and how often do you do it?"

"Why, I jump in that pond you just came out of and rinse off all this dirt and vegetation that's accumulated on me over the past cycles. Normally, I'd do it every hundred cycles like everybody else, but I slept through the last dunking."

"Why?"

"Boredom. Nothing exciting's happened here since we joined rGov, except for a visit from some ugly fellows about three thousand cycles ago. Came from a planet called Ugh or something like that. Didn't stay long, though. rGov rounded them up and shipped them off-planet so fast we never had time to ask why they visited."

Egrog gave Nick a quick look, then asked, "Would you be referring to the invasion from Grunt?"

"Might be, but Nob would know for sure. Hey Nob! Wake up!"

A nearby dirt mound stirred, and though it had no visible arms, legs, or mouth, it gave every impression of taking a big stretch followed by a huge yawn.

"Oh, hi, Phil. What's up? Did I sleep through purification again?"

"No, but we have visitors from off-planet."

"Really? Wow! It's been giga-cycles since I saw a new face. Are they doing anything, um, interesting?"

"Not yet, but they have some questions about our last visitors, and I thought you might be more helpful than me."

"Sure! Glad to help." The dirt pile called Nob shuffled closer to Phil. "Introduce me, if you will?"

"Naturally. This round-shaped fellow calls himself Egrog and says he's from gob. The short fellow is Nick, a ghoulie, and the mantid is Alice."

"I see our jabber friend has returned. Hi Silverblade!"

"Hello, Nob!" Silverblade sprawled on his stomach and closed his eyes. "Hope you don't mind if I nap for a bit. All the excitement of escaping from Grunt has me a bit knackered."

"Not a problem. Phil, what's this about Grunt?"

"These folks were asking about our last visitors and wondered if they might have been grunts. Unfortunately, I napped through it all, Nob, so I thought you might be more helpful."

"I see. By the way, you seem to have overlooked one of our guests. Who's the bipedal fellow with two heads?"

"My name's Mindy, and I'm from Earth," she said, joining the conversation. "But I don't have two heads."

"Oh, sorry! I thought those were eyes on the lump attached to your torso. I hope I didn't offend?"

"No offense taken. I think you must mean Bumpkiss. He's been resting in my bra since we left the wormgate. Fighting off all those grunts tuckered the little fellow out."

Nob perked up. "You went to Grunt? And fought a battle? Wow! Nothing like that ever happens around here. What happened?"

Egrog waddled over to Nob and said, "That's a long story, my friend, but I'll be pleased to share it. We were looking for you and went to Grunt to find out the coordinates to your planet."

"Why would you want to come here? This is the most boring place in the galaxy."

"But, don't you have eternal youth?"

"Oh sure, but what can we do with it without hands or tentacles to do anything. It all gets a bit dull after a few thousand lovely sunsets."

"What about an oral tradition of literature? Can't you tell each other stories? Or sing?"

"About what? We can't build anything, and without external appendages, we can't even fight with each other. Boring. The highlight of our lives is the purification ritual, but it only happens once a century. Take a nap, and you miss it, then it's another hundred cycles of sitting here gathering dust."

"A world without war? Not even a Saturday night brawl?" Alice asked, confronting Phil.

"Yep. Can't even throw insults at each other. Being covered with dirt makes it hard to find fault with somebody else's appearance if you follow."

"I follow. Yuck! What kind of addle-pated fudge-suckers inhabit this place? I'd shoot myself in the head if I lived here." Alice turned away in disgust.

Egrog moved closer to Nob, flattening his body a bit so that he was on the same level as the oggie.

"So, Nob, let's get back on topic. The history books recorded an invasion of a planet called Altimus about three thousand cycles ago. Think back. Could they have meant Tirnan-og? And could it have been the grunts?"

"Oh, yeah! That's the planet. Grunt. But I never heard any talk about an invasion. They did make some nice big craters we turned into ponds, but nothing significant."

Egrog twitched his eyestalks at Nick, giving him a quick wink, then focused on Phil. Grinning, he said, "That's quite interesting, my friend. Yes, indeed, fascinating info. You wouldn't happen to know how it is that you people live so long?"

"Clean living," Phil answered promptly.

"Clean living?" Egrog echoed, pink with dismay. He clearly hadn't envisioned such an impediment to immortality.

"You bet! There's nothing like a good bath in the local pond to make me feel a thousand cycles younger."

"Oh," Egrog chuckled, "you mean regular bathing. I imagine you use a special mixture when you take these rejuvenating baths?"

"No, plain water like in that pond behind you works just fine."

"But that makes no sense!"

"Why not?"

"But, surely there must be—"

Fweeee - skzzert!!

Egrog's question was interrupted by the scream of an aircar passing low overhead, followed by the mind-wrenching detonation of a stun bomb.

39

Nick fell to the ground clutching his head in agony, as did Mindy, barely aware of Silverblade leaping to his feet to face their attackers. Egrog just slumped into a puddle of twitching magenta gelatin.

"I hope this isn't more of Urk's cronies," Nick moaned, expecting the worst as a heavily-armed aircar settled to the ground nearby.

He wasn't entirely reassured when he heard a loud voice from the aircar call out, "This is Officer N'onoch of rGov. Everybody put down your weapons and lay flat on the ground! I repeat, stand down, or we will open fire!"

Nick had a burgeoning conviction that he'd soon be headed for a recivilization facility.

As the rGov agents deplaned, Bumpkiss slipped back into Mindy's cleavage, his favorite hiding spot. Before he did, he made the ion cannon disappear, though Nick couldn't figure out how he did it, as the rod was three times as long as the little kzinten. He felt a slight burn of admiration as Egrog struggled to his feet next to Silverblade to confront the agents.

"Officer N'onoch! What a delightful surprise!" Egrog said with a smile that would have been the envy of used aircar salesmen throughout the galaxy. "Now, we don't want to be a bother, so we'll just mosey along and let you get about your important rGov business."

"You're not going anywhere," N'onoch replied. "You're coming back to the wormgate station with us when we're done disarming your jabber friend. You're free to move about until then, but don't wander far. I'm getting tired of chasing after you."

"Speaking of that, officer, how did you find us? I thought the keyhole coordinates were erased when we jumped here."

"That was easy. When you keyholed off the wormgate with no apparent destination, it triggered an immediate investigation. When an unscheduled keyhole was reported on Altimus, I requisitioned a starship and jumped straight here, invoking emergency protocols so I could arrive directly in orbit. We spotted you on visual surveillance an hour ago. We'd have picked you up then, but it took some time to dismount weaponry to deal with the jabber."

Looking over at Silverblade, Nick saw that the jabber was surrounded by rGov agents and that a squad was covering the jabber with a grav-sled mounted rail gun designed to penetrate the thickest armor on a battle cruiser. Nick decided to put some distance between himself and the action and made his way down to the pond.

When he got there, he noticed Phil and Nob slide into the pond, sluicing off a century's dirt in the process.

The result was surprising.

Slow and ungainly on the ground, the oggies were sleek and graceful in the water, gliding effortlessly like mantas. With the dirt removed, their proper form was revealed, and they looked much like three-meter-wide eggs served sunny side up. Pale white skin surrounded purple bulges where egg yolks would have been.

The motion of the oggies in the water was calming, and the rest of the group soon joined Nick on the shoreline to watch them.

After a time, Phil returned to shore.

"That was great!" he exclaimed as he slid across the sand to a stone depression set a few meters from the water.

Phil hunkered down over the hollow and sighed.

"aaaaahhhhhhh..."

As he did, his central bulge shrank and changed from purple to green.

"Ew," Nick muttered, turning away. He would have stood elsewhere if he had known that he was next to an oggie latrine.

"Don't you people have refresher booths?" he muttered.

"Why would we need those?"

"Civilized beings don't pass waste in public."

"That's a pretty insensitive remark! But I guess it's to be expected from somebody with more than one sex. We don't have genitals to hide, so there's no stigma about going around naked or any bodily functions."

"Okay, sorry! But who's going to clean up your, um, output."

"rGov takes care of that."

"Huh?"

"Yeah! Well, technically, it's their robots, but they gave them to us thousands of cycles ago."

Egrog waddled over next to Nick to join the conversation. "Why would they do that?"

"I don't know. But the robots vacuum up every drop of our purple leavings."

"Odd."

Egrog gingerly extended a tentacle to the basin and sniffed at the purple fluid it contained. Then, with a grunt of surprise, he formed the tentacle into a straw and dipped it into the fluid for a sip.

Nick recoiled in disgust. "Ew! Egrog, that's gross!"

"No, my dear ghoulie, it is not disgusting. What it is, is hyper-concentrated purple glurb. Taste it yourself if you don't believe me."

"No, I think not."

"I'll try it, loverboy," Alice said, settling down next to Egrog.

Dipping a talon in the fluid, she daintily licked it clean. Then, shuddering, she stuck her proboscis in the puddle and slurped up a huge draught.

"By the Hive Mother's holy tits, Egrog's right. And this isn't just purple glurb. It's got to be a hundred times normal strength. Wow, what a flam diddle kick this stuff has!" Alice staggered, then flopped to the ground, where she lay giggling and feebly waving her feet in the air.

"What are you up to?" N'onoch yelled, running over to where the group was huddled around Phil's basin. "Stay away from that!"

"Too late!" Egrog's smile was as wide as his green-tinted body. "We might not have found the secret of eternal youth, but we found out where purple glurb comes from."

"Oh, you have, have you?" N'onoch laid his hand on his pistol. "That's dangerous knowledge."

"Er, let's not do anything hasty that I, um, we might regret!"

"I'm beginning to think I should have let Urk finish you off before taking him down on Grunt."

"Now, now, no need to get nasty. I'm sure we can work something out."

"I don't see many options for you and your friends, gobbet, besides a full memory wipe."

"How about if we promise not to tell anybody? There's no need for anybody else to know that the galactic government is funded by a highly narcotic liquid produced by oggie micturition."

"You? Promise? Do I look as gullible as your ghoulie sidekick?"

Before Nick could object to the insult, Egrog bristled and tapped N'onoch on the chest with a half-dozen fingers. "Hey, no need to insult my friend! But listen, we'll promise to keep the secret of purple glurb for a million credits apiece. And, of course, you drop all charges."

"Ha! It would be easier and cheaper to just shoot all of you and blame it on Urk."

"Aren't you forgetting something, officer?" Silverblade asked, his voice dripping innocence like a proctologist asking a patient to bend over. Nick noticed that the rGov agents had succeeded in divesting the jabber of his battle harness, but the ghoulie wasn't sure that it diminished the creature's natural ferocity.

"Like what?" N'onoch froze as he turned to look at the jabber. Unnoticed, Bumpkiss had slipped out of his hiding spot in Mindy's blouse and was now perched on the officer's shoulder.

"Hic."

"Call it off," N'onoch whispered, staring into three ruby orbs only a few centimeters from his own.

"Hic." Bumpkiss' tone clearly communicated mild distress at having to repeat himself, with strong overtones of incipient violence toward anyone so foolish as to make a sudden move toward a weapon.

"I don't think little Bumpkiss likes you threatening his friends," Silverblade chuckled, strolling over to the basin.

"Get it off me!" N'onoch said with as much authority as he could force through a windpipe constricted with fear, which wasn't much. Nevertheless, Nick was impressed with the centauran's courage, if not his wisdom.

"Perhaps if you ask him nicely?"

"Ask? The kzinten is an animal. It can't possibly understand what I say."

"Oh, but there you're wrong, officer. Bumpkiss is fully sentient, perhaps more so than the rest of us. He understands you well. It's just you who are unable to understand him."

"Really? Then what did he say?"

"He went on at length about the imminent demise of anyone who mistreated his friends. I particularly enjoyed the part about eating you from the inside out, starting with your stomach and working up through your internal organs until he reaches what passes for a brain in a rGov agent. All conveyed with a melancholy sense of the fleeting nature of life.

"All that in just one syllable?"

"Like I said, he's a good deal more intelligent than the rest of us."

"But you can understand him? Do you think you're smarter than us too?"

Silverblade snorted his amusement. Unfortunately for N'onoch, the jabber's sinuses were still damp from a plunge in the pond, and he disgorged a string of mucus that draped across the rGov agent's chest like a string of moldy, green garland.

"Oops. Sorry about that! No offense intended, officer." The wicked gleam in Silverblade's eyes somewhat undermined his apology.

"But no, I don't think I'm smarter than anybody. Except for him." Silverblade pointed at Egrog, causing the gobbet to turn reddish-brown in annoyance. "My ability to understand a kzinten comes from long cycles fighting side-by-side with our battle-brothers in the war against the dark horde on Wochness.

"Long we strived alone, and desperate was our need until the day when the crystal ships of the kzinten appeared in the sky, and they joined our cause. Together, well, that story is for another time and place. For now, it is enough for you to know that my people know the kzinten of old, long before your Galactic Empire emerged."

N'onoch gritted his teeth. "That doesn't change the situation. I can't let any of you go. If the secret of purple glurb ever got out, rGov's chief funding source would disappear. And this planet would be devastated by commercial interests fighting to gain a monopoly on it."

Silverblade laid down, crossing his legs in thought. After several moments of silence, he said, "Looks like we're at an impasse, officer. Allow me to suggest a solution."

"Which is?"

"Let the others go; nobody will believe their story anyway. Give me a ship, and I'll take the kzinten home myself."

"No! There's not a chance in a flaming afterlife that I'd give a jabber a ship, even if I had one. You'd start raiding innocent worlds, causing untold havoc and loss."

"I'll promise to leave known galactic space after taking Bumpkiss home."

"Promises are easily broken."

"I'd trust him," Nick said. "He kept his word to help us, and everything I've seen shows him to be a being of honor. Besides, it's a good choice. Solves the problem of what to do with a jabber and kzinten. And the rest of us will promise to keep silent about the true source of purple glurb if you agree."

N'onoch fumed, a process made more interesting by the continued presence of an apex predator centimeters from his face. "Even if I agreed, and I'm not saying I would, where would I get a ship? And what do I do with the rest of you?"

"!#Nick! Tell them I'll do it."

"What? Are you sure?"

"Absolutely! I'd do anything to escape the mind-numbing drudgery of my current servitude."

"Okay, I'll suggest it."

Nick sidled closer to N'onoch. "Uh, excuse me?"

"What?"

"I've got an idea. What about that transport we took from Downside to the wormgate? The AI unit running it is reliable but underutilized, and the ship itself is old enough that it would cost rGov little to acquire it."

"Are you referring to unit 30.456.7.821.32?"

"Yes."

"Hmm. That might solve another problem we've got." N'onoch gave Mindy a glare. "After transporting your missionary friend, the unit has begun proselyting other AI units with some strange religion the goofball has conceived. Not technically illegal, so we can't just delete the unit, but it's already causing morale issues, and we'd like to find a way to silence it. Sending it to the other side of the galaxy might work."

"!#Nick, you're not going to let him talk about me like that, are you? It's bad enough that rGov wants to trample our religious freedom, but calling me a—"

"Shh. Let me handle this."

"Officer, I believe 32 would be pleased to participate."

"How do you know that?"

Nick paused, realizing he'd just given away something he might have wanted to keep secret. But it was too late to change his strategy. All he could do was roll the dice, hoping he didn't crap out.

"Because I have a Qdot implant that permits communication with 32. It's been monitoring our progress ever since we landed on Grunt. Which means it also knows the secret of purple glurb. If anything happens to us, it can transmit the info to AI units all over the galaxy before you can stop him."

"What?" N'onoch visibly paled at that thought.

"It's prepared to keep quiet if you agree to the deal we've offered."

"!# I have?"

"Yes. Now hush!"

"How do I know the AI will comply?"

"AI units can't lie, as you well know. Also, it's bored. The chance at adventure is a compelling reason for the unit to keep up its end of this deal."

N'onoch chewed his lower lip for a minute in thought, and Nick noticed the frown lines on the agent's forehead deepen.

"Okay. I have serious reservations, but maybe something can be arranged under the circumstances."

"Wise choice," Silverblade murmured as Bumpkiss hopped off the centauran's shoulder, landing on the bridge of the jabber's nose. "Now, what about my friends?"

"I'm not giving them a million credits. But suppose they agree to have memory blocks installed about this incident to ensure their silence about purple glurb. In that case, I'll return them to the planet where all of this started, clear their names, and give them enough credit to resume their normal lives." N'onoch glared at Egrog. "Whatever that might be."

"Excellent." Silverblade curled up next to the basin. "How about we all stay right here until you make the necessary calls?"

"Wait a minute!" Mindy moved to confront N'onoch, her face pale. "I'm not going to have my memory wiped again. You'll have to kill me first!"

"Mindy—" Egrog tried to restrain her, but Mindy was furious, and she grabbed N'onoch by his shirt.

"No! I won't do it!"

Nick joined Egrog, and together they managed to pull the angry woman off the agent.

N'onoch straightened his uniform, then paused. From the concentration on his face, Nick was sure he was looking up something on the rGov database. "Ah, now I understand. I didn't realize who you were. You were with the Earth missionaries who were massacred on Grunt, and rGov suppressed the memories of the incident. That was for your benefit as much as the government's. Have the memories returned?"

Mindy nodded, eyes hot with anger.

"Then why in the world did you return to Grunt? And—oh my! That's why you were in the Temple of Conquest! To get the coordinates for Altimus."

"Yes. This was my one chance to be free of rGov and the church."

N'onoch nodded his understanding. "I'm sorry. I do sympathize with what you went through. But that doesn't change the situation now. This is the best deal I can offer, and I don't see where you have any viable alternatives."

"Hic!"

Silverblade sat up, eyes crossed as they focused on the kzinten balanced on his nose. "Are you sure, little one?"

"Hic!"

"Very well, you can be exceptionally persuasive when you take the time to explain yourself in detail. I'll ask."

"Ask what?" N'onoch said, baffled at the exchange.

"Let Mindy come with us. Then there will be no need to meddle with her memories."

"That's insane! It would be totally irresponsible for me to let a defenseless being travel with two of the most deadly predators in the galaxy! We lost contact with the ship transporting the other kzinten somewhere in the Orion nebula. I won't be responsible for another disaster."

Mindy walked over to the jabber and gently lifted Bumpkiss onto her shoulder. "Officer?"

"What, Mindy?"

"I'll do it. These are my friends who have fought and risked their lives for me. If you think they'd harm me now, you're mistaken. And I have to admit that I'd be sad and worried if you made me leave little Bumpkiss alone. Even with Silverblade to watch over him, he's just a little guy and needs my protection."

Nick felt his eyes bug out in amazement. He'd seen the kzinten in action, and the only creature needing looking after would be its next victim. The rGov officer clearly had similar feelings.

"Uh, that's a little hard to comprehend, given how danger-ous kzinten are."

"Only to those who mean them harm."

"Hic!"

Mindy bumped noses with the kzinten, something that still caused Nick to hold his breath in expectation of the Earth woman meeting a horrible demise.

N'onoch rubbed his face, shook his head, and sighed. "I can't believe I'm saying this, but okay. If you go on record as voluntarily undertaking this journey with them, then I'll do it. But your friends still have to get memory blocks."

Nick swallowed, then asked, "How extensive will the blocks be?"

"Everything to do with Altimus and most of what hap-pened on Grunt. Knowledge of the jabber ties too closely with your trip to Altimus to allow it to remain. We'll also remove your Qdot connection to the AI unit. That's a back door that needs closing."

"Then, I'll never see my friends again or be able to talk with them?"

"That's the deal. Unless you'd rather go through recivilization?"

Nick shivered. "No thanks, I'll take the deal. What about you, Egrog, Alice?"

"I'll do it," Egrog answered promptly. "This place is not what I expected," he shivered a bit, likely, Nick surmised, at the thought that clean living was a condition of eternal youth. "And the less I remember about the grunts, the better."

N'onoch turned to the mantid. "What about you, Alice?"

"I'll do it, but I'm not going to farking like it. Especially losing my memories of Grunt. Our escape from the mud-sucking natives and our glorious triumph over our enemies should be recorded in legend, not lost for all time."

N'onoch gave a little sigh of relief and almost smiled, a process Nick suspected rarely happened.

"Then it's settled. "

N'onoch waved his agents forward.

"We'll leave right away. A large compartment in the aircar by the pond should accommodate the jabber, Mindy, and the kzinten. The rest of you come with me."

"Wait a moment, officer," Egrog said as he waddled over to Mindy.

"I'll miss you," he said, giving her a hug with a dozen tentacles. "And you too, Bumpkiss."

"Hic!"

"I know. And I'd want to go home too if I was you. I hope it works out for you." Turning to the jabber, Egrog made an abortive motion to hug him, then stepped back as the jabber bared his teeth in what Nick considered a less-than-friendly grin. "I'll even miss you, though I'm not sure why."

"It's been an honor," Alice said, breaking the awkward silence. "To fight at the side of a warrior from legend and see our enemies fall like reeds before a storm. Even though I will lose all memory of our glory, it was still worth it." Turning to Mindy, she nodded and gave a brief salute. "You have been a valued sister-in-arms, and I salute your courage."

To Nick's surprise, Alice winked at the kzinten. "And you too, little one. Good luck finding your home."

It was Nick's turn to say goodbye, and it took him a moment to recover from the unexpected event of Alice completing two sentences without a single curse word. Stepping up to the jabber, he patted the creature's shoulder. "Goodbye, Silverblade, and good luck."

"Luck to you, too, ghoulie. May the dice always fall in your favor."

Nick grinned. "That would be a nice change!" Then, turning, he gave Mindy a hug made awkward by being half her size and his effort to keep some distance from the kzinten, who still terrified him.

"Go safely." He tried to say more, but his throat was too tight to let the words out.

Mindy hugged him back, seeming to understand his feelings. "You too, Nick. It's been a pleasure knowing you. Take care."

"Of who?"

"Yourself, silly!"

"Oh. Is that—"

"Yes, it's another earth saying." Mindy chuckled as she released him.

"I'll take good care of Mindy and the little one," Silverblade said to the group with unusual gentleness.

N'onoch put his hand on Nick's shoulder and pulled him away. "It's time to go."

Silverblade dipped his head in a bow to Nick, Egrog, and Alice, then said,

"Parting's grief may shadow friends passed in time
yet in memory, all unclouded shine."

After one last look, he followed Mindy to the waiting aircar, the kzinten perched on his head like a Maharaja riding a war elephant.

Nick glumly followed Egrog and Alice as the rGov agents led them to the other aircar. The kzinten had scared him so badly that his loins still ached from clenching them, but to his own surprise, he missed the little guy.

After boarding the aircar, Nick was separated from his friends, and he saw nothing more of them, even after the rGov starship popped through the wormhole at a wormgate station.

41

When they reached the wormgate station, N'onoch put Nick in a holding cell by himself, and it seemed like hours while he waited for something to happen.

When the cell door opened, N'onoch was outside, flanked by guards, and Nick knew the waiting was over. Whatever was going to happen to him would soon transpire.

At a gesture from N'onoch, Nick followed the silent agent through several corridors and then on a quick jaunt in one of the station's transit pods.

When they arrived at their destination, Nick paused, nervously rattling his lucky dice.

"Why are we in the med sector? Is one of my friends ill?"

"No, we're here to fulfill the bargain you made," N'onoch said, leading Nick into a white room lined with obscure devices and one oversized, well-padded chair.

"Wha...what are you going to do?"

A centauran technician in a blue lab coat answered in a voice as reassuring as an engraved invitation to Boris Karloff's castle, "don't worry, you won't remember a thing."

A second technician strapped Nick into the chair and positioned a large silver helmet covered in glowing spikes over Nick's head.

"Please, I promise I won't tell!" he squeaked pathetically.

"Of that, we can be certain," the first tech replied, reviewing his instructions on a tablet supplied by N'onoch. "But don't worry. We'll only block your memories of that last place you visited. Everything else will be intact. Unless there's something else you'd like us to block while we're at it, like an ex-spouse, a bad habit or such?"

The tech lifted an eyebrow and half-smiled at his own joke. Then he tapped a button on the side of the helmet, and Nick passed out.

42

Nick woke in an economy cabin of a passenger starship. Even if he hadn't been familiar with such accommodations, the cold aluminum walls, gray high-friction flooring, and slightly actinic smell would have clued him in.

His head was clear, but he had the odd feeling that there was something he needed to do. Suddenly it came to him, and Nick sat up in surprise. He'd been on Grunt, in a jail cell, and...now he was here. But where was Egrog? And his other friends?

Getting up, he activated the terminal on the wall at the foot of his bed. It immediately displayed the rGov agent, N'onoch.

"Hello Nick, glad to see you're awake. How do you feel?"

"I feel fine," Nick said, confused. "How did I get here? The last thing I remember was being in a cell on Grunt."

"That's not surprising. The grunts got pretty rough with you before rGov could mount a rescue. The med techs who treated you said you might have difficulty remembering what happened, and given the grunts' reputation, that's probably for the best."

"But, what happened to my friends?"

"They're all fine and have been treated and released. And by the way, we picked up the loan shark who was after you. It will be a long time before he leaves the recivilization facility."

Nick's bowels unclenched with relief. "That's good news. But what about Egrog, Mindy, and Alice? Where are they? And what am I doing on a starship?"

"As I said, they were released without charges. Egrog and Alice are on a different ship but headed to the same destination as you. Mindy recovered quicker than the rest of you and took a starliner back to Earth. I understand she plans to rejoin her church."

"She does?" Nick thought back to Mindy's fear of being recaptured by the church. The agent's comments didn't match his memory, but he thought it would be unwise to mention his reservations.

"What, uh, what happened to the kzinten?"

"Returned to its home world."

"That's good. So, what's my status? You mentioned that charges were dropped?"

"Oh yes, you've been cleared of all crimes, and the judiciary awarded you a small amount of credit to permit returning to everyday life.

"Really? That's great! But, my grav license—?"

"Reinstated. Your boss from the Vagabond got caught with contraband and confessed to framing you for the lubricant theft. You should be able to find a meaningful job again once you land."

"Land where?"

"Downside. That's where your adventure started, and we thought you might want to go back there."

"Back to Downside?" Nick was appalled. "But, that planet's awful! It rains all the time, and I don't like rain."

"It's the least we could do. The very least," N'onoch said enigmatically, then closed the connection.

Not knowing any of the other passengers, Nick spent the remaining few days of the trip to Downside eating, sleeping, and playing vid games in his cabin. He was delighted to find his backpack and all its contents intact, including his lucky dice and grav tools. He was also pleased to discover that his personal Slymebook account had been reactivated. He thought about contacting Egrog via the Stellarnet, but the ship had a hefty surcharge for connection to the net. He wasn't sure he wanted to talk to Egrog anyway, so he decided to wait until he had landed and could find a cheap connection.

After the transport touched down, he gathered his few belongings and stepped off the ship into Downside's eternal gloom.

Trotting through the downpour, Nick hopped on a slidewalk and headed out of the spaceport. It was raining hard enough to flood areas of the streets, and the only reason Nick's socks weren't soaked was that the slidewalk was elevated well above the surrounding turf.

Nick smiled. Even Downside's persistent funk wasn't enough to dampen his spirits.

N'onoch had kept his promise, dropping all charges and giving Nick transport back to Downside. And, checking the credit chip under his fingernail, Nick was relieved to verify that rGov really had cleared his debts. And they'd issued him enough credits to pay for a month's lodging at the Rigellian Arms. Things were finally looking up.

As the slidewalk carried him away from the spaceport, the flashing sign for the Blue Sky Bar & Grill beckoned like an old friend. Nick hesitated, jiggling the dice in his pocket. He had enough credit, and knew where he cold find a game just a little further on. But to his surprise, the itch was gone. Making up his mind, he slipped into his favorite dive, taking a deep breath of the musty air as he snuggled up to the bar.

The robot bartender wiped the counter clean, but before Nick could order, it placed a small box in front of him. "Good to see you again, Nick."

"What's this?" Nick asked, picking up the box and examining it.

"From a mutual friend. Can't say more. Care to order?"

"Yep! I'll have a glorpburger and wiffle-fries with a mug of Glurb ale."

"Make that two," Egrog said, oozing onto the barstool next to Nick. "I've been looking for you, buddy. I've been here almost a week, and I was hoping you'd get in touch when your ship landed."

After a few moments of arctic-class silence, the gobbet continued, "Look, I know you're mad at me. I'm sorry about the mess on Grunt. I didn't expect it to play out like that."

Their drinks arrived then, and Nick took a long pull before finally saying, "Egrog, it's my own fault. Whenever you offer to help me, I end up in worse trouble than when I started. And a quest for the secret of eternal youth? I'm embarrassed that I fell for that."

Egrog took a sip of his own drink. "I can't blame you, bud. Truthfully, I'm not even sure what happened on Grunt. Memory's a bit fuzzy. Say, what's in the box?"

"Don't know. The bartender says it's from a mutual friend but won't say who."

"Why don't you open it and find out?"

Nick turned the box until he found a finger-shaped depression on one side. Recognizing a biometric-coded access pad, he pressed his thumb on the depression, causing the box to open with a click.

Inside was a small green disk, identical to the one 32 had used to insert a Qdot under his skin.

Nick paused to wonder who might send him such a thing or why, but the only being he could think of was 32.

Shrugging, he pressed the dot against his forearm and felt a slight tingle as the Qdot and its interface slipped beneath his dermis. A moment later, he sensed the device connecting to his nervous system.

"!#Nick! I see you have arrived safely on Downside and have received the present I left for you."

"Hi, 32. What's up? And where are you?"

"We're on the outer fringe of the Orion-Cygnus arm of the galaxy."

"We? Who's with you?"

"Silverblade, Bumpkiss, and Mindy. They all say 'hi.'"

Nick scratched his head in puzzlement. *"Who's Silverblade, and what are you doing so far out from the civilized worlds?"*

"That, my friend, is quite a story. But before I start, you might want to think twice about drinking that Glurb ale…"

(finis)